PURSUING
CARRIE

Jenn Hype

Pursuing Carrie

ISBN-13: 978-0-692-55554-5
ISBN-10: 0-692-55554-4

Book design by J. F. Rountree
Cover photograph © conrado/ShutterStock.com

www.jennhype.com
press@jennhype.com

First Edition March 2016

Printed in the United States of America
10 9 8 7 6 5 4 3 2 1

For some other people
Just because

CHAPTER 1
CARRIE
PRESENT DAY

"Bitch doesn't belong here if she can't understand why Gerard is so important to me!"

Joe's date had just stormed out of my apartment, and I was honestly a little surprised she did it with all of her hair in tact with how angry Stacy was. She didn't escape unscathed, though. Blondie McBigBoobs would have a dildo shaped bruise on her face for a few days.

"Stacy," I said calmly, placing a hand on her shoulder. When I had her full attention, I spoke slowly to make sure she understood. "If you ever get in my cabinet and steal one of my dildos again, I will stab your tit while you sleep. Furthermore, you will be replacing both dildos - the one you took, and the one you just threw at Joe's girlfriend."

"She's not my girlfriend," Joe chimed in. I was tempted to turn around just so he could see me roll my eyes, but Stacy was facing him and did it for me.

"Why do I have to buy you two dildos? What's wrong with this one?" Stacy bent down to pick up the light-up pink vibrator I hadn't even had a chance to use. She pressed the power button and it started twisting and turning, which now that I really looked at it, seemed like it might actually kinda hurt.

I made a disgusted face at her when she tried to hand it to me. "I'm not sticking that in my bat cave when it's been manhandled by someone else's hands, hit Joe's skank girlfriend - who probably has a long list of STD's - in the face, and then rolled around on my floor."

"She's not my girl-"

"Make Joe replace it! He's the one who brought his slut girlfriend without telling anyone. I wouldn't have had to throw it at her if she wasn't such a dumb twat, so really, it's all Joe's fault."

Everyone, myself included, turned to look at Joe who was standing with his hands up in the air and his mouth gaping open. "Hey, don't blame Stacy's unique brand of crazy on me. No one deserves to have a dildo thrown at them, so that's on Stacy."

A bright pink blur flew past the side of my head and landed squarely in the middle of Joe's face. "Fuck, Stacy!" Joe's hands flew to his face, covering his nose and muffling his voice. "What the hell did you do that for!?"

"Because you're wrong. Some people do deserve to have dildos thrown at them. At this moment, you were one of them. Seeing as how I had a dildo handy, I figured it prudent to chuck it at your dumbass face."

Stacy stormed out of my apartment, Chad hot on her heels. It wasn't uncharacteristic of her to get ridiculously, over-the-top dramatic about things, but she actually seemed mad. When five minutes passed and neither of them returned, the silence in my apartment grew quiet. None of us understood what had just happened, and we were all a little too stunned to speak.

"Can somebody get me some fucking ice for my nose or something?!"

I hopped into action, grabbing a bag of frozen peas from my freezer. It had been in there God knows how long, but I didn't think it mattered if vegetables were expired when it came to icing an injury so I handed them over. Joe winced when the bag touched his face, and I winced right along with him when I saw the swelling at the bridge of his nose.

"Well, I'd love to stick around and endure some more weird shit, but I think Adalyn and I are going to head out." My brother, Ian, leaned down to give me a quick kiss on the cheek before slipping his arm around Adalyn's waist. "Thanks for dinner, sis. Our place next time."

They tossed out quick goodbyes to Joe, which he returned with a grunt. Once the door was closed behind them I plopped down right next to Joe.

"Suck it up, buttercup. You're a cop. I think you can handle a little bump on your nose."

Joe glared at me over the bag of peas still pressed firmly against his face. I didn't even try not to laugh, because that shit was funny.

"Okay, pretty boy. Let me take a look." He let out a low, annoyed growl, but I just rolled my eyes and pulled the peas away. "The swelling is already going down. I doubt you'll have much more than a little bruising." I lightly brushed my fingertip across his nose, pulling away when he winced. "Sorry."

"It's fine. My pride is hurt more than my face. I've had a lot of injuries in my life, even some pretty strange ones, but this has to be the most embarrassing one. The guys at the station are going to give me so much shit about this."

"So don't tell them," I offer with a shrug. It's ridiculous advice really. Knowing Stacy, she's already sent out a group text from Chad's phone with a detailed review of what happened. We both laugh spontaneously, undoubtedly thinking the same exact thing. Once the laughing dies off, a comfortable silence spreads between us.

Ironically enough, being 'comfortable' around him makes me uncomfortable. Every interaction between us up to that point had been laced with tension, which ended with us fighting or kissing.

Shit.

Thinking about the last time we kissed while he's sitting inches away from me on my couch was a horrible idea. I didn't know if the change in the atmosphere was all in my head, or if Joe noticed the room suddenly heat up and the air thicken to an unbearable point. Really, I had no clue what was going on in his head, and I was too chickenshit to look at him to find out.

I stood up, needing to put space between us, trying to figure out a polite way to get him the hell out of my apartment so I could breath again. Being polite wasn't my forte, and I needed something to do while I came up with a strategy to get him out without coming across as a bitch, so I headed to the kitchen to start picking up.

Leaving the room silently was probably weird, but I couldn't not be weird right then if my life depended on it, so I focused on gathering all the plates on the table. I didn't even notice Joe had walked in until I heard the kitchen faucet turn on. It startled me so much that I dropped a plate. I dropped down to my knees and started picking up the pieces scattered all over the floor, but I'd only managed to grab a couple before I went airborne.

"What the hell are you doing? Put me down!"

Joe had me gripped under my arms from my behind as he walked a few steps before plopping me down on a chair.

"You made dinner, I'll get the mess. You have a dress on, you don't need to be on your knees picking up sharp pieces of porcelain."

He was being all police man-y with his brusque tone and puffed out chest. It had me equal parts intimidated and turned on, my body completely on edge the entire time I watched him grab a clean wine glass from a cabinet and fill it with Moscato. I downed it in one drink and swiped my upper lip with my hand in the most unladylike fashion imaginable. Joe quickly refilled it, and I took an appropriate sip that time.

Once he accepted that I wasn't going to argue or throw something at him, he checked a few places before opening the door to my utility closet and pulling out a broom and dustpan. I sat quietly while he searched for soap and other things, never once asking me where to find something. The need to just get up and do everything myself had me twitching in my seat, but every time he opened a cabinet he looked over at me, like he was just waiting for me to react.

I wasn't going to give him the satisfaction. It felt like a lose-lose situation, but at least the option of just sitting on my ass meant I got to sit on my ass.

I finished off another glass of Moscato, and he was refilling it before I could even reach for the bottle. Our silent exchanges continued until the kitchen was spotless and I was decently buzzed. Joe put away the last dish and tossed the dishrag over his shoulder, and the entire scene was so domestic. So *normal*. It had me wanting things I had no business wanting, just like every other time I was around Joe.

Shit.

SEVERAL MONTHS BEFORE THE APTLY NAMED "DILDO DEBACLE"...

"You're killing me with that outfit, Care. Did you actually buy that at a store, or did you just dig it out of the back of some old grandma's closet? I bet if I sniff you right now you'll smell like moth balls."

Stacy has been my best friend since we were just out of diapers, and giving me crap about my choice in clothing was nothing new, so I didn't even bother responding or trying to defend myself. She knew why I dressed this way, and while she understood my reasons for the most part, it didn't keep her from ragging on me every chance she got.

"I love you, Carrie, I really do, but you make the worst wingman ever," Stacy complained as we walked into the crowded bar. "You do know we're here to see a band and hang out, not have a PTO meeting, right?"

I glanced down at my clothes, and looked back at her. I wasn't dressed any more conservatively than normal, and I thought I looked cute in a sophisticated, librarian kind of way. I mean, yeah, I wasn't sporting hooker heels and a mini skirt like Stacy, but it wasn't like I was wearing a moo-moo, either.

Admittedly, my black slacks, sensible heels and light pink cardigan that was layered over a cream colored lacy tank did make me look more suited to be attending a business meeting than a night out with my girlfriend, but I was comfortable and that's really all that mattered to me. I had been tempted to wear a string of pearls just to piss Stacy off, but I didn't really want to spend the entire night being subjected to her sarcastic jabs towards my wardrobe.

I wore the same amount of makeup I usually did, which was just a light layer of mascara and a pink gloss, but it still brightened my face enough to give me less of a 'walking corpse' look. I usually kept my long, auburn hair straight and sleek, and tonight was no different. I pulled it into a neat ponytail that tied at the base of my hairline and hung down past the middle of my back.

I wouldn't be turning any heads, that was for sure, but that had never been my priority. Truth be told, if it were my choice, I'd be sitting at home having a Criminal Minds marathon while binging on trail mix. Not technically junk food, but it had chocolate, and it was the worst I'd allow myself to eat when it came to cheating on my diet.

I was only out with Stacy because I hadn't seen her in forever, and I was curious to meet this Joe guy she'd been spending so much of her time with. From the way she'd described him, he sounded delicious enough to eat, but she swore emphatically that there was nothing other than friendship between them. That alone was enough to pique my curiosity, but I sensed there was more going on than she was letting on. And since she was being so tight lipped with all the details, that meant I'd have to find out on my own.

Stacy had talked to me about Chad, and having known Stacy my entire life, I knew tonight was only going to add to the shit storm happening between the two of them. He was a police officer who had arrested her not long ago for public intoxication, which is how she met Joe, who was Chad's partner.

From what I'd heard, it sounded like Stacy had met her match in Chad, and they were both too stubborn to admit they liked each other. I was even a little excited to finally get to witness one of their infamous pissing matches in person. Of course, I'd only heard the stories from her perspective and Stacy had a tendency to seriously exaggerate, so who knew how the night would go.

I knew the moment Stacy spotted Chad after we walked through the door. Her entire body tensed as she stopped dead in her tracks. What I hadn't expected was how cordial her and Chad were acting towards each other after she made her way over to him and introduced me. He spared all of two seconds of his attention in my direction, before turning it right back on Stacy. I had to bite back the smile that tugged at my lips from watching how adorably obvious it was that they were attracted to each other, despite how hard they were trying to hide it.

Chad was exactly as I'd pictured him. Stacy had

been extremely accurate with her depiction of him. He was every bit the stereotypical hardass cop, if you were going based on looks alone. His shoulders were broad and his biceps large enough that I probably couldn't fit my hands around them. He wasn't in uniform or anything, but he looked so much the part that there was probably no way he'd ever be able to do undercover work. Everything about him screamed law enforcement.

Stacy and Chad chatted briefly, then she and I made our way to another part of the bar while Chad went to retrieve the mysterious Joe. I was racking up the balls at a pool table when a deep voice carried through the room, cracking a joke about being careful with his balls. I looked up to see a gorgeous face smirking at Stacy, and considering he was standing next to Chad, I deduced that the face belonged to Joe.

Joe gave me a once over that, if possible, was even shorter than the one Chad gave me. I observed the three of them bantering back and forth, trying my best to focus on the pool table. Stacy never bothered introducing me to Joe, and admittedly, I thought Joe was a little rude for not taking it upon himself to try and speak to me. If he was truly as close to Stacy as she made it seem, then you'd think he would try a little harder to get to know me.

All I really knew of Joe, other than how much Stacy adored him, was that he was a bit of a slut. Two seconds in the same room with him and it was easily understandable based on his good looks and the obvious charm. Of course, he didn't bother to waste any of that charm on little old me, which was perfectly fine with me.

I didn't doubt for a second that women threw themselves at him everywhere he went, and maybe he had expected me to do the same, but hell would freeze over before that would happen. As little respect as I had for men who couldn't keep their dick in their pants, he was young and single and really, what red blooded male wouldn't sample the varieties as much as possible? Just because I would never be one of the women throwing myself at him didn't mean I couldn't understand where they were coming from. If it weren't for my rules, then Joe would definitely be the type of man I would enjoy a roll in the sack with.

The next couple hours were enjoyable, despite how often it felt as if all three of them forgot I was even there. Every time I would chime in with a joke or comment, they would all turn and give me a surprised look, like they wondered where the hell the strange voice was coming from. This type of situation wasn't uncommon, especially when I went anywhere with Stacy. She commanded the attention of everyone around her, while I preferred to be standing on the sidelines, enjoying the show.

I wasn't anti-social, I just wasn't over-the-top, in-

your-face outgoing like Stacy. If I wanted anyone to focus their attention on me, I'd have to fight for it around
her, so it was a good thing I never really cared either
way. I got all the attention I needed when I was on stage
and the spotlight was on me. I'd been dancing my whole
life, and nothing compared to those moments of soul-
baring vulnerability when all eyes were on me, watching
as I offered up a piece of myself each and every time I
took the stage.

When we tired of our game, we took seats at a table,
and Chad and Joe finally seemed to acknowledge that
there was a fourth to their group. Chad tried to engage
me in conversation, but I was there to find out information, not provide it, so I was always quick to steer the
topic back to the other people at the table. Stacy and
Chad eventually broke off and left me alone at the table
with Joe, where we sat for several minutes in uncomfortable silence.

Joe was picking at the label on his beer bottle, fidg-
eting and acting like he was nervous. I chuckled quietly to myself, wondering what the hell he was nervous
about. I had been all but invisible to him all night long,
and he didn't seem the type to get nervous talking to anyone. I looked at him more closely and realized he wasn't
nervous; he was just uncomfortable. He was trying to focus on his beer, but his eyes kept darting up to the other
women around us. Each and every one of them would

wink at him, not even subtly, apparently assuming that I was not his date. Or maybe they just didn't care.

"Don't let me keep you if you'd like to go socialize. I'll be fine here," I spoke up, breaking the silence. His head whipped to face me, guilt written all over his face. Did he think this was some kind of double date? God, I hoped not. Surely Stacy wouldn't give him that impression. I smiled sweetly at him, wanting to ease his mind, only it must have had the opposite effect because his frown deepened.

"No, I'm cool," he replied, clearing his throat. He averted his eyes, but kept his head pointed towards mine, and I took a good look at his face for the first time. He was what most would call a 'pretty boy.' He had a youthfulness to his features, with his dark hair just a little too long and his full lips a light shade of pink, as if he'd just spent the last hour making out on a couch in his mom's basement.

He wore a tight white cotton polo that fit snuggly, showing off his arms that were toned in the way you would expect a runner or swimmer's to be. A broad chest tapered down to a slim torso, leading down to his well fitted jeans, which I couldn't see now, but had gotten a good view of when we were all playing pool.

I would have bet money that his ass was tight and delicious enough to take a bite out of. Not that I would ever be doing the biting, but my active imagination was thankful for the mental images being conjured up as I continued to take in Joe's appearance.

Joe cleared his throat suddenly, and I blushed when I realized I'd been caught staring. His innocent smirk told me he didn't mind being ogled, so I did one more obvious once over, just for good measure. I didn't want him to think I was too intimidated or embarrassed to be able to appreciate a beautiful man when he was sitting right next to me. Much to my surprise, though, the way his lips twitched up on one side into a sly grin made my stomach stir more than the visions of him naked I'd just been having.

When I finally tore my eyes away from his mouth and back up, we sat for several seconds in some sort of stare down. It was bizarre and made me want to shift in my seat, but I fought the urge and held my ground. I cocked my head to the side and narrowed my gaze at him curiously, which resulted in a chuckle from Joe, who ended up being the one to tear his eyes away.

Joe went to speak, but someone shouting his name from across the room drew his attention away, and he excused himself to go speak with someone standing on the dance floor. I wasn't sure where the relief came from when I noticed the person he was speaking with was a man, but I pushed that aside and looked around, realizing Stacy had disappeared.

I stood up to go looking for her, and after one lap

around the outside perimeter of the bar, I spotted her on the dance floor. I looked over just in time to see some guy take a swing at Chad, and the next several minutes passed by in a crazy blur. I wasn't sure how I even managed to make my way back over to the pool table, but once I was a safe distance away, I turned back to see Joe inserting himself into the middle of a fist fight.

Joe said something that seemed to calm Chad down, and the bouncer escorted the other guy out of the bar. Chad didn't have a mark on him, and I was itching to know the details of what would cause that kind of outburst.

I saw Stacy head towards the back patio, and I started to follow her, but someone standing just a few feet away stopped me dead in my tracks. When his eyes met mine, feelings of betrayal and humiliation hit me hard enough to choke the life out of me.

He took a step in my direction, so I turned quickly on my heel and bolted through the crowd to the bar. I needed a drink, and I needed it stat if I was going to survive being in the same place as Brad for very long.

I threw back four shots in quick succession, and they went down my throat and hit my empty stomach before I even had a chance to taste them. I wiped my upper lip with my index finger and spun around, discreetly scanning the room for Brad. Not because I *wanted* to see him, but because I wanted to *avoid* him.

I spotted him in a corner, talking to a beautiful girl, and she was laughing at something he said and flirtatiously touching his arm. He smiled back at her, and even though it was quick, I saw his eyes dart over to me briefly. With the alcohol slowly seeping into my system, my pain quickly turned to anger, and I pushed away from the bar and moved towards the dance floor.

A new song started, and my hips started to sway to the music when a hand snaked around my stomach and pulled me backwards. I expected to be pulled into a hard body, assuming a man was just wanting to dance with me, so I didn't resist. Problem with that was, no one was waiting to catch me, and I stumbled.

The hand moved from my waist to my elbow, and that's when I noticed it was Joe, and he was pulling me towards the exit.

"Hey, hey, hey. Where do you think you're going?" I yelled over the loud music.

"Stacy left. She asked me to get you home," he responded, not bothering to look back at me as he continued pulling me towards the door.

"Well too damn bad for Stacy, because I'm not ready to leave and I don't need a babysitter. I'm a grown ass woman and I'm capable of calling myself a freaking cab."

I stumbled again, only that time it was lack of coordination causing my clumsiness. Damn alcohol. Hopefully Brad wasn't witnessing this.

Pfffft. Who the hell cared?

I danced through several songs, my arms raised and my eyes closed, and I just assumed Joe had left since he hadn't tried to drag me out of the bar again like a caveman. When I started to sweat, I ripped off my cardigan, earning a few catcalls. The lacey tank underneath was pretty transparent, and everyone was given a good glimpse of my black, lacy push-up bra.

Downfall to being a dancer - my big boobs. I mean, they were nice boobs, filling a D-cup quite nicely. But dancers weren't supposed to have curves, and there were many times growing up when I had to actually duct tape my boobs to my chest to make them look smaller. The only part of my body that hadn't suffered while I was watching my weight all these years was my chest, which meant I had zero curves. That's great and all if you're a principal dancer in a ballet, but not so much if you were just a normal girl wanting to feel sexy.

I twirled my cardigan over my head like a lasso and tossed it into the crowd, and the response I got was heady. It was surely the alcohol, but I didn't care. I needed to feel good about myself, which I never did when Brad was around, so any positive attention I could get I would take it.

A petite brunette came over to me and started dancing, and when I put my knee between her thighs and started rolling my hips, the men around us went wild. I hit my limit when she tried to shove her tongue down my throat, but she didn't get offended when I pulled away. Instead, she took my hand and led me over to a table, where she climbed onto a chair, pulling me up with her.

We stood on the table, shaking our asses for a few songs. She was wearing a skirt so short that it covered absolutely nothing, giving everyone in the bar a good look at what she was wearing underneath. Which was nothing, by the way.

I felt my body start to overheat, and I knew I needed to sit down or drink some water, or both, but I wasn't ready to stop dancing. So instead I kicked off my shoes, dancing barefoot on the table, and pulled my hair up higher into a messy bun. My skin was slick with sweat, and I seductively ran my hand down my neck, over my chest and down my stomach.

I bent my knees and crouched, rolling my hips and sticking my ass out on the way back up. I opened my eyes long enough to regret it, because the first thing I saw was Brad. And he. looked. pissed.

Well, fuck him! I knew I was acting completely out of character. I knew everyone in the bar tonight thought I was some kind of attention-seeking whore and most likely an easy lay, but that's Brad's way of thinking. Not mine. He was always such a judgmental ass, and I'd be damned if I let him continue ruining my life.

After I closed my eyes again, I felt myself being lifted and thrown over someone's shoulder. Before I could even find out whose shoulder I was on, I was being ripped off of it and pulled back into another body. I was the little metal ball in the middle of a real life version of pinball.

"What the hell, man? Back off. C'mon Carrie, I'm getting you out of here."

"Fuck you, Brad!" I shouted, wiggling and jerking my body. I knew it was Joe's arms around me, and while he smelled and felt amazing, all I wanted was to lunge at Brad and scratch his eyeballs out. My efforts were futile, but I kept fighting with everything I had to try and squirm out of Joe's hold. I probably looked, and sounded, like a drowning cat with all the shrieking and my sweaty, disheveled state. No fucks did I give in that moment.

Brad's head jerked back in surprise. "What's happened to you, Carrie? This isn't you. You're going to regret this tomorrow. Just let me take you home." He sounded genuine and looked concerned, but the asshole was really good at playing the part when necessary and I wasn't buying it.

Instead of continuing to argue with him, I turned around in Joe's arms and snaked my hands behind his neck, pulling his mouth down to mine roughly. I was angry and wanted to hurt Brad, and it was shitty of me to use Joe like I was, so I started to pull back when I felt Joe's lips freeze against mine.

Only when I started to pull away, Joe's hands moved from my back to my hips, pulling me closer to him. His lips started to move, and the kiss went from angry and reluctant to mind blowing. I don't know how long we stood there, necking like a couple of horny teenagers, but I do know I never wanted to stop.

I'd never been kissed like that. It was sensual and toe curling, and when his tongue darted out against my lips, seeking entrance, I happily acquiesced. If it were possible to have an orgasm from kissing alone, then I would have right then. I swear, it was like my whole body lit on fire. I was so desperate to have more of him, feel his hands all over my body, and I didn't care that we were in the middle of a crowded bar.

My hands roamed eagerly all over his body, grop- ing and scratching every available inch. My libido was possessed and my body reacted accordingly. Any other moment I would have been horrified at my actions, but the way Joe's mouth tasted lightly of beer and pepper- mint was intoxicating. I felt completely out of control, but instead of it being terrifying, it felt freeing.

If Joe hadn't broken the kiss and pulled away when he did, then I have no doubt I would have started tearing at his clothes.

Brad cleared his throat behind us, but my glassy

eyes were too entranced by Joe's darkened stare to turn around. When he cleared his throat again, Joe tore his eyes from mine and narrowed them at Brad.

"I can get her home," Joe said sternly. It wasn't an offer; it was a command. I was still locked on Joe's face, so I didn't miss the tick of his jaw when Brad spoke up.

"Not necessary. Carrie is my responsibility; I'll be the one taking her home."

It was loud in the bar and I was more than a little drunk, so I could have imagined it, but I swear Joe growled when Brad grabbed my elbow. Joe put a possessive arm around my waist and pulled me further away from Brad. Hard. I felt like a rag doll, being jerked back and forth while they had their little pissing contest. Normally having two men fight over who got to boss me around would annoy the piss out of me, but I could feel Joe's abs through his shirt, so all usual reasoning flew right out the window.

It clicked in my head exactly what they were fighting over, and there was no way in hell I was leaving with Brad. I didn't really want to leave with Joe either, or at least I didn't *want to* want to leave with Joe, and I knew when to admit defeat. It was my own damn fault for drinking too much when I knew I couldn't tolerate it, anyway.

Not wanting their arguing to continue, I slipped my hand into Joe's and started towards the exit without sparing Brad so much as a backwards glance. When the chilly night air hit my hot and sweaty skin, my body shivered hard enough to rattle me. The alcohol sitting in my empty stomach churned, and the nausea had reality reentering my addled brain.

It was like I'd been in a trance for the last half hour, and I yanked my hand from Joe's. I did it because I needed to cover my mouth, a subconscious effort in trying to hold back the vomit, but I didn't miss the dirty look he gave me when I pulled away. Part of me wanted to reassure him I wasn't being rude, another part of me wanted to tell him to get over himself, but the drunk part of me told the other parts of me to shut up and focus on not retching on the sidewalk.

I kept my mouth clamped shut all the way to Joe's truck. It wasn't until I was standing next to it that I felt brave enough to speak without fear of throwing up on him.

"Why did Stacy leave?"

"Hell if I know," Joe said, sounding frustrated, as he tried to reach around me for the handle to the passenger side door. I stepped to the side, blocking him, and tried to figure out why he sounded so damn snippy. Did he not feel the electricity between us like I did when we were kissing? Was my ability to interpret the situation too distorted because of the alcohol and stress of seeing my ex?

He mimicked my stance, crossing his own arms, and

stared me down. I couldn't tell if it was challenge in his eyes or annoyance. Was he angry that I kissed him? I had no idea what the hell was going through his head, and I wanted to flick his forehead and tell him to stop acting like a child. All I *actually* did was hiccup and sway.

He rolled his eyes and mumbled something under his breath about me not being able to hold my liquor, then gripped my elbow to steady me while trying to pull open the door. Him standing so close to me reminded me of just how much his kiss had affected me just minutes ago, and the thought of being alone with him, especially this pissy and asshole version of him, made the bile rise back up in my throat.

I made a feeble attempt to push away from him, and summoned my inner bitch.

"I'm a big girl, I can find my own way home. I'll just call a cab, no reason for you to leave on my account." My little argument would have been much more effective without all the hiccups, but when he let go of my arm I considered it a win. I started to walk back towards the bar, but Joe only let me make it about five steps before he grabbed my elbow again and spun me back around. I looked down to where his hand was on me, and he tightened his grip.

"Sorry, no can do, half pint. I've been put in charge of getting you home safely, and that's exactly what I'm going to do. So be a doll and hop in the cab for me."

The charm I'd heard in his voice earlier when he'd spoken to people was there, but it sounded forced. *Asshole.* Even after that spectacular kiss he still acted like I wasn't worth his time.

Joe opened the door to the truck, but I just stood there glaring at him. I didn't expect for one second for him to view me as anything other than Stacy's quiet and plain friend, but I did not appreciate him talking to me like I was a child. Granted, my behavior tonight had been far from mature, but who the hell was he to judge me based on his first time meeting me?

Instead of continuing to argue, I turned on my heel to leave. He still had a firm grip on my elbow, and when I felt my body jerk back and my feet kick out from under me, I yelped. I had about two seconds to digest the fact that I had apparently left my shoes in the bar before I was airborne, and before I knew what was happening, I was being deposited into the front seat of Joe's truck. He even managed to buckle my seatbelt for me and make his way around to the driver's side before I could get out a protest. My options at that point were jump out of a moving vehicle, or suck it up and let Joe take me home. Since I didn't think ruining my career would be worth it just to get away from the bossy man next to me, I opted to stare out the window and sulk.

The only conversation that took place on the quick drive were my directing Joe where to go to find my place.

I dozed off a time or two, Joe waking me once every few minutes for more directions. Once he pulled up to my building I debated thanking him for the ride, not wanting to be rude, but also still mad at him for forcing me into his truck to begin with. He saved me from having to decide by getting out and coming around to open my door and speaking first.

"Want me to walk you to your door?" There was a suggestive glint in his eyes. Was this asshole actually hitting on me? His personality shift was so quick it had my head spinning, and next thing I knew I was throwing up on the sidewalk.

Okay, maybe my head was spinning because of the shots I'd drank and not because of Mr. Hyde here, but still.

My hair was up so I didn't need him to hold my hair back, not that he would have anyway. I stood up and cursed myself for my dizziness causing me to sway. Joe put an arm around my shoulder and my vomit breath had me feeling too self conscious to yell at him to get off, so I let him walk me to the front door of my building.

He opened the big glass door and stepped in behind me, and I had a momentary lapse in sanity where I thought he was trying to follow me to my apartment. My sober self would have known better than to assume he would flirt with me, even if I *hadn't* just thrown up very close to his shoes. But I wasn't my sober self. I was my drunken, stupid self, so I grabbed his hand and walked over to the security guard of my building who was stationed behind a shiny oak desk.

"Miss Drake, lovely to see you," the old man said politely. I had no shoes on, vomit on my chin and I was a sweaty mess, but if he noticed he didn't show it.

"Mr. Martins," I started, taking a pause to hiccup. "This is Joe…" I trailed off realizing I didn't know his last name. Joe started to speak up but I kept going. "Joe whats-his-face, and I want him put on my 'never is he ever allowed in this building ever' list."

Mr. Martins' eyes widened and Joe snickered behind me. "Um, I don't think you have such a list." I lifted my hand to wave dismissively, but Joe's came with it, because while I was telling Mr. Martins to never let Joe in, I was apparently holding his hand. I quickly let go and shuffled away from him.

"Okay, well make one, and put him on the top. Always a pleasure, Mr. Martin," I said with a shaky nod. Joe had moved to block my path to the elevators, and I tried to push past him. My shoulder bumped his, and while he stood firmly in place, it knocked me off balance just a little. My 5'2" and hundred and five-pound frame were no match for his very tall, muscular one. I heard him chuckle behind me as I found my balance, thankful to have my back to him so he couldn't see the blush creeping up my neck as he yelled after me. "See you soon, half pint!"

CHAPTER 2
CARRIE

It's incredible how much can happen in such a small amount of time. Since making a drunken fool of myself at the bar the night I met Joe, I'd managed to avoid him, but it hadn't been easy. Between Adalyn, my brother's girlfriend, going missing and a new business agreement I was working on, time had been a rare commodity. Adalyn was okay, but it was a big hoopla of drama, which resulted in Ian's ex-girlfriend getting her ass kicked, to which I was delighted.

For the first time in a week I found time to go running. I walked past Mr. Martins and smiled back when he said good morning. He hadn't mentioned the little scene I'd made since it happened, and I was grateful to go on pretending as if it never did.

Once inside my place, I headed straight into the kitchen to make an energy shake. Sometimes I wished I could just eat a bagel for breakfast instead of some organic, vitamin infused crap that tasted as bad as it looked, but until I decided to give up dancing, I didn't really have a choice.

I hated eating in front of people. Everyone assumed I had some kind of eating disorder or had body issues just because I ate healthy. Honestly, though, for all I knew, maybe I did have a problem. I always assumed that if it weren't for dance then I would be just as unhealthy as the vast majority of people, but truthfully, I liked the way eating healthy and working out made my body look. The only part of my body that wasn't ultra small were my boobs, which I still maintained a love-hate relationship with.

Stacy attacked me every time I complained about how big my boobs were. And I mean *literally* attacked me. The last time we went bra shopping security had to pull her off of me when she tackled me in the dressing room when I casually remarked about how annoying it was to have to buy D cup sized bras. We were both down to our knickers, so the staff, shoppers and security guards were all given quite a show while we rolled around on the floor in Victoria's Secret. If you knew Stacy then it wouldn't surprise you to hear that instead of getting in trouble for making a spectacle, the security guards both asked for her phone number. I walked away with Stacy's bite marks on my shoulder while she walked away with a date.

Story of my life.

I was rinsing out my glass after choking down my shake when I heard my phone ringing on the kitchen island behind me. A glance at the screen told me it was Stacy. I still needed to get my shower and was tempted to just let her go to voicemail and call her back when I got out, but it was early in the morning and Stacy almost never called this early unless it was important. Only when I answered my phone, it wasn't Stacy on the other line.

"Carrie?"

"Yeeeahhh?" I dragged the word out, confusion clear in my tone.

"It's Joe. Sorry to call so early, but I have a favor."

An hour later I was inside of Stacy's apartment, waiting for her to return from the police station with Joe. According to Joe, Stacy had been hurt the night before by some thugs and had refused to be seen by a doctor. He didn't give me any details, and honestly, I was in too much shock to even think to ask for more information.

The entire time I rushed through my shower and getting ready, I ran through the worst case scenarios of what happened over and over again in my head. I wished I had Joe's phone number so I could text him all the questions I'd thought of once I processed the little amount of information he'd given me.

Stacy's apartment was on the outskirts of the city like mine, so thankfully the drive was short. I'd had a key to Stacy's apartment since she moved in, so I let myself in and started cleaning up her place, killing time until she got back. I'd always been motherly over her, it was just my nature. Stacy liked to think she was always taking care of everyone else, but it was more in a protector kind of way. I had always been the one to keep her in line when things got chaotic for her, which was often, considering how spastic she was.

Stacy's sloppy ways usually grated on my nerves, but I was thankful for the distraction while I waited for her to get back. I was finishing up the last of her dirty dishes when her door opened, and Stacy wobbled in, being supported by Joe. Her face was a mess and she was clearly in pain, but I managed to keep my cool long enough for her to sit on the couch, before following Joe out into the hallway to hopefully get more information.

"What the hell happened to her!" I hadn't meant for my question to come out sounding accusatory, but I knew Joe had been with her the night before, so I couldn't for the life of me figure out how Stacy could have gotten hurt so badly when she was with a cop. Joe looked surprised at my outburst, but answered me calmly.

"She got attacked at the club last night."

"No shit, you already told me that. How did it happen? You were with her! Why aren't you all busted up?!" I was yelling still, but it was more of a whisper-yell. I didn't want Stacy to hear me through the door.

"I was inside the club when it happened. It's a long story, but I think it'd be better to hear it from Stacy. Trust me, I feel like shit for not being there when she needed me. If it will make you feel better though, I'll gladly stand here and let you scream at me some more."

His lips twitched like he was fighting a grin, and I wanted to be pissed at him for being able to smile at a time like this, but I found myself biting back a grin of my own. It didn't matter that it had been months since that night we kissed, my body still responded in exactly the same way. The memory of that kiss kept me up at night, haunting my dreams, and never in my life had I been so physically affected by a man. We hadn't talked about it, which could partially be from my avoiding him, but he didn't seem like the guy to blink twice at some drunk chick throwing herself at him, anyway. I probably wasn't even a blip on his radar, as far as exciting events, which was both relieving and depressing at the same time.

Not to mention how he'd turned into an ass and then I'd had him banned from my building. I supposed that probably had something to do with neither of us making any real attempt to see each other again.

"Give me your phone," he demanded. Instead of grabbing my phone out of my back pocket, I just crossed my arms and glared at him. He rolled his eyes and held his hand out, like that would be enough to convince me to follow orders. I started to ask him why when he let out a frustrated sigh and reached around me, dipping his hand in my back pocket and pulling my phone out himself, causing a slight shiver to course through me from the feel of his fingertips on my ass. I wanted to yank it out of his hand and shove it back in my pocket, just to get him to do it again, but he was already typing away on it before I had the chance.

"I'm programming my number in here for you," he said as he locked the screen and held it back out for me. I was still dazed from my unwanted reaction to him, and when I didn't move to take it back, he reached around again and put it back in the pocket he'd taken it from. He lingered longer than necessary, and I had the good sense that time to jerk away from his hand. Joe chuckled, looking entirely too smug, and it pissed me off that he knew the kind of effect he had on me.

"Don't know why you're putting it in there. I don't want it," I said stubbornly. I wanted to smack the smirk off his gorgeous face. If it weren't for my hang ups, I would throw myself on him whenever he looked at me with that crooked grin that had women tripping over themselves to get to him. He damn well knew it, too, which made me want to react in the exact opposite way.

"It's so you can text me updates about Stacy. I'd stay home with her today, but I have some partnering issues to deal with at work, so I have to go in. I'm worried about her." His smirk disappeared and his expression turned thoughtful. I uncrossed my arms and almost instinctively reached out to hug him, wanting to comfort him, which was bizarre because I wasn't a very physically affectionate person. Plus, I barely knew him. But his worry for Stacy was sincere, and I appreciated that he cared.

"Oh, well that's fine. I'll make sure and keep you updated, don't worry," I said, shifting uncomfortably. With all the smirking and ass grabbing I had assumed he was hitting on me, which was naive and ridiculous. Someone like Joe would never be interested in someone like me.

Where the hell did that come from?

I never worried about what others thought of me, or whether or not someone found me worthy of their attention. In general, I didn't want their attention. What was it about Joe that had me thinking like an insecure girl crushing on some teen heartthrob? So what if he wasn't interested in me. I wasn't in him, so you know... it worked out.

The fact that I was disappointed that he wasn't interested in me wasn't something I was going to be addressing any time soon, or ever, so I'd just have to figure out a way to shove that little issue into a box and lock it away.

It took me by surprise when Joe pulled me into a hug and pressed a kiss to the top of my head, which was easy for him to do since my height put me right below his chin. I stood there, stiff and with my arms straight down by my sides, not returning his hug. It was an affectionate gesture; the kind a dad would give to his little girl. The kind my dad used to give me before he abandoned us. The kind of affection that once brought back warm memories, but now only served as a reminder of just how insignificant I was.

Laughter rumbled in Joe's chest beneath me. "What? You can make out with me in front of your ex, but you won't hug me when we're alone?"

I could have laughed it off. I could have flirted. I could have gotten angry. I could have done *anything* except what I actually did.

"What are you talking about?"

Oh man...not reacting to the look on his face took superhuman acting powers, for which I should have been given an Academy Award. He looked like someone had ran over his dog, told him Santa wasn't real, and that the Berenstein Bears *was* actually spelled Berenstain Bears all at the same time. It was adorable and funny as hell. I didn't like it when he was adorable. Made it harder to dislike him.

"You kissed me. At the bar."

I scrunched up my nose and shook my head, and managed to not fist pump the air with how freaking awesome I was doing at keeping my cool.

"Pretty sure I would remember something like that," I said seriously. Joe actually looked confused for a minute, like he was considering the possibility that he actually imagined it. He searched my face, probably looking for a sign that I was messing with him, but I was stoic.

The longer I remained entirely unreadable, the more confused Joe got, and the more adorable he became. And the more I kept thinking the word 'adorable' the more I wanted to punch myself in the face, because adorable on Joe was actually endearingly sexy.

"No, you kissed me." His ego was hurt, that much was clear. I wasn't trying to be a jerk, I was just nervous and reacted stupidly, but I was down the rabbit hole so I decided to see it through. Plus, he seemed like his ego could stand to be taken down a notch.

I feigned a stunned look, then looked sheepishly at the ground. "Sorry," I said just above a whisper. "I guess I don't remember because of how drunk I was." I gave him an apologetic shrug, and I swear I watched his whole world go crumbling down around him.

Yeah, his ego was seriously massive if he found it *this* hard to believe that I could forget kissing him when he knew I'd been drunk off my ass. Did he really think that his kiss was so powerful that it could withstand the mind erasing abilities of drugs?

Despite the lack of room in the hallway due to his large, albeit shrinking, ego, I wanted him to kiss me again. To be determined to make *this* one memorable, and for a second he looked like that was exactly what he was going to do. He stared at my lips, his tongue darting out to wet his own, and I sucked in a quick breath between parted lips. My body swayed in his direction all on it's own, and Joe leaned his face down to mine, our noses brushing lightly.

I closed my eyes and waited to feel his lips on mine, but when seconds ticked by and he still hadn't kissed me, I opened my eyes to see what he was waiting on.

Then I watched the asshole's whole face light up with the biggest shit-eating grin, and froze in shock when he gave my chin a playful swipe with his knuckles, before smiling at me affectionately and saying "thanks for helping, half pint," and walking away. I watched his form retreating down the hallway, and would have been embarrassed when he looked back and caught me staring, but considering how obvious it was that I'd been put in the friend zone with him, it didn't really matter.

I reminded myself once more that it was a good thing that Joe apparently viewed me as a precious little girl, even though I was only a couple years younger than him. Even if for some strange reason he was attracted to me, nothing would ever come of it, for a plethora of reasons. None of which would matter later when I was lying in bed, picturing Joe's hand on my ass and the feel of his hard body against mine, as I pleasured myself. And that's all it would ever be, just him and my imagination, because I wasn't capable of anything more.

I took a few seconds to shake off my little interaction with Joe, knowing Stacy would notice my strange behavior if I didn't push him from my thoughts, before going back inside.

CHAPTER 3
JOE

Cursing myself under my breath as I made my way to my truck, I couldn't believe how narrowly I had escaped, only seconds away from humiliating myself.

Forgot? She freaking forgot *that we kissed? What the hell kind of crap is that?*

I really thought she was messing with me at first. At least, I hoped she was messing with me. That night she was drunk, sweaty and dressed more like she was on her way to a country club than a bar. But dammit all to hell if she wasn't sexy as fuck anyway.

I stayed back and let her have her fun, but there was no way I was going to leave her there. I'm not an asshole. I will be the first to admit that yeah, I didn't really notice her much at first. Okay, pretty much the entire night. I was getting vibes from the start that my normal charming ways wouldn't work on her, so I just kind of kept to myself instead of engaging her.

Then she took that damn sweater off and all rhyme and reason left me. Her skin was glistening with sweat, her eyes closed with a smile on her lips that she wore simply because she was having a good time, not because she was trying to pretend. Something had changed in her when she started dancing, and the rigid and quiet girl she started out as turned into a desirable temptress.

She moved fluidly, and instead of her body moving to the music, it almost looked like the music was following her. It was captivating, and even though I knew she was one hundred percent off limits, it didn't keep the guy downstairs from noticing.

When her small hands lifted in the air above her head, I pictured both of them wrapped around my cock, her fingers probably too small to reach all the way around with one hand. And when she turned her body in my direction and I caught a glimpse of her hardened nipples through her flimsy shirt, every inch of my body stiffened. Men all across the bar were noticing the same things I was, and jealousy began brewing something fierce.

I didn't particularly like feeling jealous, and never really had before. Not when it came to women and feeling jealous in a possessive way. I didn't do long term relationships and any girl I spent time with knew the score, and in general I didn't sleep with a woman more than once. Not because I didn't desire to, but because in my experience, the more you slept with someone the more attached they got. With no feelings involved to mess up the whole thing, I managed to stay friends with pretty much every woman I'd ever been with.

So if ex lovers found themselves in a monogamous relationship and had to disappear from my life, I waved goodbye and moved on. I never missed them or regretted not making a move. Never felt any kind of ownership over them, or any other kind of boyfriend type feeling. But knowing these men were ogling Carrie, lusting for her body the same way I was, made me unreasonably angry. I had no right to her. Hell, I'd been ignoring her all night, acting like a shallow asshole and not even trying to get to know her.

I forced myself to look away when she started dancing with another girl who tried to make out with her, and I planned to hide in the shadows until she was ready to go. But when her whole demeanor changed and I saw pain and anger flash in her eyes, I knew I couldn't hold back any longer. I didn't know what had caused it, but my protective instincts kicked in and I was rushing to her side before I had a chance to talk myself out of it.

I reached her just in time to get that asshole ex of hers to back off. Of course I didn't know who he was at the time, but it was obvious enough that he was the cause of her change in mood. I could tell in the few sentences we exchanged that he was a self-serving prick, trying to lay claim to Carrie and pretend to be some kind of knight in shining armor for her. He didn't care about Carrie, he just cared that she was getting attention from the men in the bar. I had no doubt that he would not have been a gentleman if she had left with him, and she would most likely have woken up regretting her night.

My intentions might not have been any more noble

than his, but I didn't have a history with her that was making her nails dig into my arm hard enough to break skin. No, her anger was directed solely at him, so if he thought for one second I was going to let her leave with him then he was fucking nuts.

Her kissing me caught me off guard in the worst way. As soon as her soft lips touched mine and her delicate hands wrapped around my neck, I wanted to devour her. I hesitated, though, knowing that she was only kissing me to make that douche wad jealous. It was a bad idea to make out with Stacy's best friend, and I had every intention of pushing her away and telling her so.

But then *she* tried to pull away, and Joe junior didn't like it one bit. A heartbeat later our mouths were moving and her hands were exploring me in ways that were supposed to be reserved for the bedroom. My body and mind warred with each other, going back and forth between doing the right thing before things got out of control and wanting to say consequences be damned and take her home to my bed where she could continue all the work her hands were doing, minus the clothes.

My whole body sparked to life and reacted in ways to her that I didn't understand during that kiss. Pulling myself off of her was literally painful, but when dick-breath cleared his throat, I found the strength to pull back. I could feel her staring at me, but I couldn't look at her. I knew what I'd see, and it would break my resolve, which was already paper thin.

Seconds later we were outside and she's pulling away from me, like she couldn't get away from me quick enough. A cold reminder that I was right and she had only been using me to make her ex jealous. It shouldn't have bothered me. A hot girl making out with me at a bar and not expecting anything from me should have been a great end to the night, but it wasn't. I was irrationally angry, and offended, and on the verge of doing something incredibly stupid.

Like scooping her up in my arms and doing it again when no one was around, just to find out if I reacted the same way to her the second time around.

Her bitchy attitude helped me keep it in my pants. Not because it was a turnoff, but because I wasn't one to force myself on someone, and she was making it clear that she didn't want to be anywhere near me. I figured she was just pissed about her ex and was taking it out on me, but a new emotion overtook me the whole drive to her place, and it felt a hell of a lot like insecurity.

I was brooding the whole drive, but she was such a feisty little firecracker the whole time that I found my bad mood slipping. Even when she would wake up for only a few seconds to tell me when to make a turn to get to her place. She was half asleep and still snapping at me, and fuck me, but it was cute as hell.

I didn't think I'd ever noticed a woman being cute

before, and glancing over at her tiny body curled up into a ball with her head cradled in her hands while she snored lightly brought a whole other onslaught of emotions I didn't recognize. I resisted the urge to reach over and push a strand of hair off her face, because if I was being totally honest with myself, I was just looking for an excuse to touch her.

And damn, I wanted to touch her. More than just her hair or her cheek, though, and I had a feeling that one small touch wouldn't be enough. It was a bad idea for a million different reasons to pursue anything with her, especially when I didn't know how she felt about casual sex, but also because of our mutual friends.

Plus, if I made a move on Carrie and it pissed her off, then Stacy would have my balls. I could stare down the barrel of a gun and not flinch, but the thought of pissing off Stacy made my whole body shudder.

By the time we made it to her apartment, which didn't take nearly as long as I wished it would, her hair and clothes were rumpled and she had a small amount of dried drool on her chin. Even with tired eyes and her skin sticky with sweat, all I wanted in that moment was to kiss her again.

She fought me getting out of the truck, she fought me while she was puking, and she had me banned from her building. And I still wanted to kiss her.

And *now*...now I find out she doesn't even *remem-*

ber the kiss? I thought she was avoiding me because she was embarrassed, but finding out she simply just *forgot* about me? That stung. Bad.

After that night I didn't set out to pursue her, happy to give her space to recover, leave her wanting more. I figured we would run into each other from mutual friends, and having never really pursued a woman, I thought my odds of getting another shot with her would be better if I let it happen organically.

I didn't even contemplate the possibility of her not *wanting* a repeat. It was only about thirty seconds, but it was so earth-shattering that it had been about the only thing I could think about since that night. To find out that she didn't even remember the kiss that had rocked my world had me feeling ten shades of pathetic.

Even more pathetic than those needy guys who went around begging women for a date, because I had gone and surpassed them. I'd spent an embarrassing number of hours pining over a woman who had all but forgotten me. Correction - *literally* forgotten me.

I'd turned down every woman who made advances on me since that night, not wanting to replace the memory of her lips on mine with someone else's. I was such an idiot for letting a random girl I didn't even know completely change me, all from one stupid kiss.

Well, now that I knew where she stood, I would be able to move on. No sense in continuing to obsess, and I was probably blowing things out of proportion anyway. I was off work today, having requested off knowing my emotions would be all over the place anyway just because of the date. The anniversary of my parents' death.

Yeah, that was probably it. It wasn't Carrie, it was just me being lonely and projecting onto her.

It was a bullshit excuse, but one I was willing to accept if it meant not adding to the pain and loneliness of the day. I may not have known what the hell to do about Carrie, but there was one thing I knew, and it was how to remedy feeling alone.

I had every intention of going out and getting laid, but by the time I made it back to my house I was beat. I could have just picked one of the girls lounging in my pool when I got there, but I was too tired to even eat, let alone have sex. Sex had never been as simple as a physical release for me, and I was in no frame of mind to please a woman right then. So instead of getting my mind off of Carrie with another woman, I fell onto my bed and passed the fuck out.

By the time I woke up, the sun was going down. I checked my phone to see if Carrie had text...*you know*... about Stacy, but she hadn't. I could hear the makings of a party starting in my backyard, but I didn't feel like mingling. Truthfully, my ego was still bruised from the blow it took earlier, and I needed time to feel sorry for myself before facing people.

An hour later, I'd done two hundred pushups, showered, done a load of laundry, and checked my phone five thousand times. I still hadn't heard from Carrie, and I knew she would contact me if something was wrong, but I needed an excuse to see her again. Actually, what I needed was to stay away from her, but I'd already made up my mind at some point while letting my mind drift during my tedious distractions.

If she didn't remember our kiss, it was simply from the alcohol. She needed to kiss me sober, and then she would feel the same way I had. In the least, maybe I would realize kissing her wasn't as great as I made it out to be in my head and I could finally forget about it. Either way, it sounded like a solid plan to me.

I pulled out my phone and shot Carrie a quick text, checking in, before starting my truck. She responded almost instantly.

Stacy is asleep. I'm heading out now.

Took you long enough. Been waiting for an update all day.

I didn't mean to come across irritated. *Dammit.* I should have thrown one of those little emoji guys in there. I'd never considered how a text came across to someone on the other end, and living in the land of I-don't-know-shit was exhausting. I ran a hand through my hair and watched a little bubble pop up, indicating she was typing a response, feeling way more anxious than necessary to read whatever she said next.

Calm your pants, pretty boy. Stacy is a handful. I couldn't even go to the bathroom without her yelling for me. If I didn't have time to eat or even sit down for two seconds all day, then it would make sense that I didn't think about texting you.

Ignoring the way her saying she hadn't even thought about me stung, I sent her a text asking how I could help, then waited. Nothing. So I sent out another, offering to bring her some dinner. Nothing.

Screw waiting around, I was just going to go to her. She said she was heading home, and she lived about twenty minutes from me, so I headed her way. She wasn't there when I pulled into her parking garage, which was concerning because she only lived fifteen minutes max from Stacy's place.

Another thirty minutes went by before I saw her car pulling in. She didn't notice me, and even through her tinted windows I could see how tired she was.

I made my way towards her car, which she'd parked about ten spots down from mine, and watched her look at her phone and roll her eyes before tossing it into her purse.

Stubborn woman. She wasn't even going to reply to my messages.

I stood right outside her door, and she never once noticed me. I could have been a mugger holding a gun to her head, and she would be oblivious. I was going to have to talk to her about the dangers of being out at night and not being aware of your surroundings. Later. I wasn't there for educational purposes. Unless me teaching her exactly how hard it would be to forget another kiss with me counted as a learning experience.

I started to greet her, but her tiny body slammed into mine before I could get the words out. She let out a high pitched squeak and fell backwards against her car, dropping her keys and setting off her car alarm.

We both bent to reach for them at the same time, and it wasn't until her hand touched mine that she even looked at my face. I pulled the keys from her grip and turned off her car alarm while she stared up at me from her still crouched position.

When she finally stood, it hit me once again just how small she was. I had to be more than a foot taller than her, because even with her back ramrod straight, I still had to look almost straight down to see her. I hadn't really had time to take in her appearance earlier, but I noticed she was still wearing the oversized sweatshirt that hung off her shoulder over a pair of sinfully tight jeans with furry boots.

"Why the hell aren't you answering my texts, Carrie? You said you were heading home almost an hour ago and you live fifteen minutes from Stacy's apartment. I've been waiting here, worried, for over a half hour." Yeah, okay, I was being a giant dick, but I'd been worried. She was so damn stubborn, ignoring my texts and forgetting my kisses. Plus, it wasn't fair for a woman wearing bummy clothes and no makeup to look so damn irresistible.

"Uh, okay where to begin..." She trailed off, tapping her finger on her chin like she was trying to figure out how to respond. Then in the blink of an eye, her whole body went rigid and her eyes narrowed on me... and damn, did she wear angry well. It was *hot*. "First of all, don't sound irritated with me when you're the one who showed up at my apartment acting like a creepy stalker - *uninvited*. Second of all, not that it's any of your business, but I hadn't eaten all day so I stopped for a smoothie. Third of all, you asked me for an update, I gave you one. Whatever follow up messages you sent weren't relevant."

She put her hands on my chest and tried to push me away, which was laughable really. I wasn't a bulky guy, but I was seriously way bigger than her. I watched as she pouted adorably and huffed in frustration, and there was no way I could avoid smiling. *So damn adorable*.

"Carrie," I said in my cop voice that I reserved for delinquent juveniles when they needed a lecture. "I'm a cop, it's my job to protect and worry about people, especially when it's someone I care about. I'm sorry if you felt like I was being pushy or nagging, but I just needed to make sure nothing was wrong."

She wasn't buying it. "I told you nothing was wrong before I left. There was nothing else to worry about."

"You didn't answer me, I got worried."

"You could have just gone by Stacy's to check on her instead of coming to my apartment for an update if you were so worried."

"I wasn't worried about Stacy; I was worried about you." She looked shocked at my confession, which confused me. Why was it so hard to believe that I would be worried about her? Yeah, we weren't close or anything, but I was a decent guy *and* a cop. It's my *job* to worry about people. "You said you hadn't eaten or had a chance to rest all day. I was worried you fell asleep at the wheel or something." The vulnerability I'd seen seconds before disappeared, and I saw her fists clench out of the corner of my eye.

"Yeah, well I'm not a child, I don't need you to worry about me. Just because I'm small doesn't mean I'm weak. I can handle a day with my best friend, who I've known a hell of a lot longer than you, by the way. I've also been driving for over ten years and have somehow managed to make it back to my apartment every night all on my own without getting lost or scared or crying out for mommy, so maybe you should worry about the people who actually need help instead of babying Stacy's friends."

She pushed me again, and this time I moved out of her way. She took fast, sure strides away from me, and I knew I should just let her go. I *knew* that, but my legs apparently didn't, because I was moving and sidled up next to her in just a few steps.

When we got to the door of her building, I followed her inside and she stopped at a desk to talk to a man guarding the entrance. It wasn't Mr. Martins from that first night, and he paid no attention to me, instead focusing on the tiny spitball marching towards him. I wasn't entirely sure Carrie knew I was standing there, since she never once acknowledged that I was even following her. Until she spoke to the guard, that is.

"Fred, I need you to do me a favor and escort this man out of the building," she told him with a firm nod of her head. I was already holding up my police badge before his eyes made it over to me, and I almost felt bad for the guy. He was obviously torn. He had a very angry little woman in his face, and I had a feeling he was trying to decide which was a worse fate - trying to force an officer out of the building, or getting kicked in the nuts by the tiny, yet terrifying, tenant.

When he didn't move to follow orders, and instead gave her an apologetic smile and slowly backed away, she turned to face me, saw me holding up my badge and growled. Like, loudly. It echoed in the large lobby, and I was a little shocked that such a large sound could come out of such a tiny body.

She stomped over to the bank of elevators that were about four feet away from where I was standing, pushed the number eight, and turned to face me. The anger in her face was gone, and all that remained was exhaustion. It was clear all the fight had left her.

"Listen, I'm sorry for acting ungrateful. Thank you for being worried and making sure I'm okay, that was very thoughtful of you. I'm not normally such a bitch. Okay, that's a lie, but I've been trying really hard to not be like that anymore and just two minutes near you and I'm falling back into old habits. So, if you'll forgive me for behaving so juvenile, I would be very appreciative. However, I am very, very tired and don't have it in me to finish this tug-of-war we seem to have going. So tell me what it will take to make you go away."

CHAPTER 4
CARRIE

It might not have seemed like it, but I was trying. I really was. But I had nothing left. At that point, I seriously wondered if I would even make it up to my apartment without collapsing. I'd been pushing myself too hard, I knew that, but admitting it didn't change anything. I had the biggest project of my career demanding all of me, and I was already running on empty before I went to Stacy's.

I never really used to care about hurting people's feelings, and I know that made me a bitch, but I didn't care. I'd lost too many people in my life, and if someone couldn't stick it out through my bad side, then good riddance. At least that's how I'd always been, up to the point where I treated Adalyn so horribly when I first met her. She was a whole lot like me in the pushing people away department, and once we reconciled I decided to face the error of my ways and try to be nicer.

I was doing a shit job at it, if Joe's crestfallen expression was any indication. Stacy had been telling me for months how great of a guy he was, and I should have listened. He was just concerned about Stacy's friend, and I was making it into something personal. I was letting my attraction to him affect my ability to read a situation, and now I'd gone and hurt someone very important to my best friend.

Joe gave me a sullen nod, looking a little like a puppy that just got kicked. I wasn't sure when we had started migrating towards each other, but he was only inches away from me for some reason. Going against my instincts, I reached out for him, touching his forearm with my hand. It was a light, friendly gesture, and it shouldn't have sent sparks shooting through my fingertips. Joe gave me a sad smile that I was pretty sure was supposed to be reassuring.

"It's no big deal. I'm sorry I pushed, I can get overbearing in my efforts to look out for people I care about. Ask Stacy, she'll tell you all about it," he said, giving a small, forced laugh.

"I get it; Stacy is the same way. I can see why you guys are such good friends. You're a lot alike. You are a good friend for watching out for me. You know, for Stacy. If something happened to me on top of everything, it really would have taken a toll on her. So...thanks."

Joe opened his mouth like he was going to say something, but snapped it shut, grimacing. He stared at me for a second like that, frowning, and it was awkward. Then he shook his head, put his hands on his hips and looked down, smiling at the ground.

"Get some rest, Carrie. I'll see you later," he said with a glimpse in my direction before walking away.

Then he was gone.

"Well, that was bizarre," I muttered, pushing the number for my floor again since the elevator had come and gone during our little exchange. Fred, the doorman, was watering a plant, keeping one careful eye on me. No doubt my little outburst probably freaked him out. I'd have to bake him some cookies or something. Well, I'd have to buy them, because I had no idea how to bake.

I didn't even get my clothes off before I collapsed in the bed, and within seconds, I was out.

"Five, six, seven, eight," I counted off from my place at the front of the studio. My dancers were exhausted, but they were as committed to this gig as I was, so giving them a day off would be a waste of time.

I was dying to jump in the routine. Part of the reason I opened my own studio was so I would have the opportunity to dance more, but a career as a dancer wasn't realistic, and even if I had made it, the lifespan of said career would be short. One injury and I would be out of the game, so I figured I would dance until I couldn't, and then just do choreography and teach.

This new business opportunity wasn't what I had envisioned for my modest little studio, but I couldn't pass it up. It would be very lucrative, which was a goal as a business owner, but it wasn't my main motivation.

The main appeal was the steady work my dancers would get from it. It would mean helping some of the girls get out of the strip club I often recruited from and give them a chance at a real job. The bad part was that it would mean I had to stick to the role of choreographer and entrepreneur instead of getting to dance.

And I really wanted to be able to participate in this one. Maybe down the road if everything went through I would have another chance, but for now, it felt like I was stuck on the sidelines. Story of my freaking life.

I reminded myself again that this new job wasn't about me, and it could change things. It could make an impact. And I still couldn't believe how it fell into my lap. Okay, not fell. More like it was firmly planted in my lap thanks to my big brother Ian recommending me, but I'd still gotten the opportunity because of my reputation, not his. That meant a shit ton of pressure was piled on top of an already stressful opportunity.

After a few more run throughs of the routine, we quit for the day. My dancers groaned, and they may not have wanted the break, but their bodies needed it. I couldn't afford for one of them to get an injury right then. Part of my job was to look out for their best interest, and working them to the bone didn't do anyone any good.

Just as everyone was filing out of the studio, Stacy came strutting in.

"Wuddup, slut?"

"Only you would think 'slut' is an affectionate way to greet a friend, Stace."

"Whatever, I just call 'em like I see 'em."

"Alright, pot, what do you want?" I asked, crossing my arms. She quirked an eyebrow at me. "Pot," I said, pointing to myself, then "kettle," pointing at her. She just rolled her eyes.

"So what's up with you and Joe?"

Her question shocked me. It was not at all what I was expecting.

"Um, nothing, why?" I started throwing my stuff in my bag, just for something to do. If anyone could get the truth out of me, it was Stacy, but I wasn't ready to face it yet.

"Joe has been acting weird, and I'd bet my left tit that you're the reason."

"But your left tit is your favorite one!" I gasped dramatically, then rolled my eyes when she responded as if I'd been serious.

"True, which proves just how confident I am that I'm right."

"I don't know what to tell you. Sorry." I shrugged and walked over to the wall to flip the lights off before heading out for the night. I'd actually planned to stay and dance a little, but with Stacy grilling me about Joe, all I wanted was to escape.

"Look," Stacy said as she gripped my shoulders,

forcing me to face her. "I'm sorry I haven't been around. I know you've been busy too, but we haven't hardly seen each other. I know something is going on between you and Joe, because you're both avoiding each other and it's making my life freaking difficult. So whatever it is, if you won't tell me, can you guys just fix it?"

She was right and it made me feel like shit. I'd been using this new potential deal as an excuse for avoiding everyone, just on the off chance I'd run into Joe. What made me feel more shitty than anything else was that I couldn't even tell Stacy that. I didn't understand the feelings I was warring with when it came to Joe, and I knew Stacy would blow it out of proportion and turn it into a much bigger deal than necessary.

So I was attracted to him? So what? He was really freaking hot, and anyone with a set of eyes would be able to tell you that. Considering his reputation for being a charismatic playboy, it shouldn't surprise anyone that his charm had gotten through my walls as well. As tough as I tried to be, I was human like everyone else. I could deny things to myself, but it didn't change the outcome, it just prolonged it.

Eventually I was going to have to face Joe and face my growing attraction to him. Nothing could happen. Ever. I had strict rules, and doing anything at all with Joe beyond a friendly handshake would be violating every single one of them. I was at no point in my life to risk opening up to someone. The price of a broken heart was more than I could afford, and while I didn't suspect Joe had any intentions of doing anything other than getting under my skin, and maybe my clothes, it didn't matter. He didn't have to be invested in a relationship. I was fully capable of screwing up my own life without his help.

Looking at Stacy, seeing the disappointment and hurt written all over her face, I had a decision to make. I could find a way to fight this pull I was feeling towards Joe so that I could see my friends, or I could risk losing the few people in my life that I let myself love.

"Listen," Stacy said, pulling me from my thoughts. "I know you have your own shit going on, and I appreciate all the time you've spent running with me and helping me train, but I'd like some real time with you. Everything right now is kind of fucked up, and as much as I really don't want to talk about it, I could use my best friend right now."

I sighed, throwing my bag over my shoulder. "I really am exhausted. Let me go home and get some rest and see how I feel. I promise I'll make the effort to come by tonight, okay?"

Stacy didn't respond, she just shook her head and left. She was disappointed in me.

Yeah well, you're not the only one.

I never made it to Stacy's that night. I had laid down to take a quick nap, setting my phone to wake me up in a couple hours. Only I slept right through my alarm. I was sleeping while thugs attacked Stacy in her own apartment, nearly raping her until Chad barged in and saved her.

There were no words to describe the guilt I felt when Adalyn showed up at my door, crying hysterically, dragging me out of my apartment and to the hospital. If Stacy hadn't been her normal sassy self, then I might have fallen apart.

Stacy getting beaten half to death wasn't even the biggest news that day - I was going to be an aunt. Adalyn was pregnant, and my big brother had gotten engaged. And damn, was Adalyn a hot mess. More of a mess than Stacy, which was surprising considering how together Adalyn always seemed. Pregnancy hormones were apparently her Kryptonite, because they had turned her into an entirely different person. I'd grown to love her personality. She was normally so fierce, an even bitchier version of me, but all pretty much everything made Adalyn cry now. Literally everything.

As strange as that new development was, I still couldn't believe I was going to be an aunt. I was still processing that information, trying to focus on the excitement and not the fear. I mean, it wasn't like I was the one having a kid, so it shouldn't have freaked me out so much.

Stacy's attack was weeks ago. Time had been flying by so quickly with all the drama in our lives. I had stopped avoiding Joe and I'd seen him on occasion, but he'd grown unusually cold towards me. Gone was the flirting and panty-melting grins, and the Joe who didn't notice my existence was back.

I wanted to feel relieved about that. I should have felt grateful. But all I felt was angry, rejected and very, very confused. I had no right to feel angry or rejected, or anything at all really since there had never been anything between Joe and I. Mostly all we'd ever done was fight, or at least I fought while he bossed and did something that beared a marking resemblance to flirting. One drunken kiss does not a relationship make, so him moving on from...whatever we were doing...it shouldn't have bothered me.

Well, everyone was coming to my place for dinner that night, so it would be a good opportunity for me to prove to myself just how little I cared about Joe's lack of interest in me. Chad and Joe were partners again, having had a falling out over Stacy a while back, and now they were reconciled once again. Stacy and Chad had gotten over their games and senseless drama, and were now living together. And my big brother was getting married and having a baby.

It was time for everyone to celebrate, and I was

happy for the distraction of being hostess. The gig my studio had been working towards had been pushed back a month, so we were getting a small reprieve from our grueling hours of rehearsal, and I'd had much too much time on my hands.

All the planning and pep-talking in the world couldn't have prepared me for seeing Joe walk through my door with a date. I pasted on the fakest smile I could manage and forced myself not to look back as he walked in with the bustiest blonde you could imagine. Seriously, they were so huge they should have their own zip code.

No one knew about what happened between me and Joe, not that there was much to tell. For all they knew, maybe we just didn't get along, which wouldn't be surprising considering how different we were and how difficult I was to get along with in general. So I was forced to pretend like I didn't care at all that the man I'd been lusting after for months, despite my efforts to not let my mind wander towards him, had walked into my apartment with a busty bimbo.

Okay, maybe she wasn't a bimbo, and I was just being a judgmental bitch.

"So like, Cassie," blondie said to me at the dinner table.

"Carrie," I corrected through gritted teeth and a fake ass smile, hoping like hell it wasn't obvious how badly I wanted to smack her in her face.

"Right, so anyway, thanks for having me over and stuff. But um, do you have any normal food?"

She was twirling her hair around her finger and chomping on gum, I kid you not. She looked at the food spread out in front of her like it was laced with arsenic, and for a second I kind of wish I'd known he was bringing her and I might have actually considered poisoning her. Not enough to kill her, but enough to make her sick enough to have a reason to get her the hell out of my apartment.

I opened my mouth to tell her if she didn't like the food being served at a dinner she wasn't even invited to then she could...

"Darcy, it's fine, I'll take you somewhere when we leave," Joe whispered to her.

I clenched the table cloth in my lap, my nails digging into my palm, knowing that all eyes were on me. This was exactly the type of situation that would normally set me off, because tolerating ungrateful bat snatches was not my forte. But tonight wasn't about me, it was about celebrating my friends and family, so I bit down on my tongue hard enough to draw blood and ground my teeth hard enough to chip a tooth.

"So Chad hid Gerard from me," Stacy said, putting the attention on her. I exhaled deeply and she winked at me.

Thanks for the save, sweety cakes.

"Is that like, your dog, or something?" Darcy asked her, showing just how much she didn't belong at the table with us. We all knew who Gerard was. When Stacy ignored her, she raised her hand like a freaking toddler, and we all just stared at her until she finally spoke up. "Um, how can he steal a person? Isn't that, like, kidnapping?"

"No, Gerard is my dildo. My favorite one, actually. And this pecker head got jealous of the time I was spending with Gerard and freaking stole him." Blondie blinked, then blinked again, then turned to face Joe.

"Is she serious?" Blondie asked him.

"Um, hello, I'm right here," Stacy said, waving her hand in Blondie's face. "You can ask me. And yes, I'm serious." Stacy turned to face Chad. "Give him back, Chad, or I will follow through on my threat."

"I really don't want to talk about this at the dinner table," Ian chimed in.

"Can't you just get another one?" Adalyn asked Stacy.

"I'll just steal that one, too. She doesn't need a dildo when she has me. It's insulting."

Stacy rolled her eyes at Chad, and went back to eating. "Whatever," she said with a mouth full of food. "I'm getting him back. And when I do, you'll rue the day you stole him."

"I'm not ruing anything."

"I rued the day I walked in to find Stacy getting intimate with Gerard. The scars from that day still run deep," Adalyn chimed in.

"I'm sorry, are we still talking about a dildo?" Blondie asked, dumbfounded.

"His name is Gerard," Stacy snapped.

"What was the threat?" Joe asked.

"I'd stop putting out," Stacy explained seriously.

The whole table, minus a confused bimbo, burst into a fit of uncontrollable laughter.

"Yeah, good luck with that, Stace," I said, trying like hell to avoid meeting Joe's gaze from across the table. He looked so damn good, and the jealousy raging inside of me at the sight of him with some tramp, made me almost forget all the reasons why I couldn't just tear my clothes off and take him there on the table.

"What's the longest you and Chad have gone without sex since you started actually dating?" Blondie made her disgust clear when Joe asked his question. For someone so slutty looking, she was acting very uptight.

"I don't know, a few hours?" Stacy said with a shrug.

"You stole him from me to begin with, Stacy," I teased, though it was the truth. "I'm afraid I have to agree with Chad on this one. I don't see why you even need him if you're getting it that often."

"You want him back?" Chad asked me. Stacy and I

both yelled "no!" at the same time.

All through dinner the conversation about Gerard continued. People started taking sides, and by the time we made it into my sitting room after cleaning up, it had turned into a pretty heated argument.

"Okay, okay. Maybe both teams should split up and make a list of the reasons they feel they are right. We can have a debate, maybe take a vote. If Chad's team wins, Gerard stays hidden. If Stacy's side wins, Chad has to give him back."

That was my brother - always trying to mediate and make something ridiculous into something logical.

I watched out of the corner of my eye as Blondie whined to Joe that she wanted to go. He looked uncomfortable, like he didn't want to leave but was afraid if he told her no then she would cause a scene. Before he could say anything, Stacy was running out of the room.

When she ran back in, I saw my keys in her hand.

"No!" I yelled, sprinting after her as she ran towards my bedroom. She slammed the door in my face just before I got there, and I heard the lock turn. There was one of those little keys to open locked doors on the frame, but I had to pull a chair out of the guest room to be able to reach it and by the time I got the damn door unlocked, she had my special cabinet wide open.

"Dammit, Stacy! What are you doing!?" I shrieked, which of course made everyone else come running. So then we were all standing in my bedroom, staring at my little makeshift sex closet.

"What the hell, Carrie? Do you own a sex store, or something?" Chad asked.

I threw my head back and groaned. I wasn't embarrassed of all my stuff, but I didn't necessarily want a room full of people looking at it all, either. Plus, Stacy was already digging through everything, and I had no idea what she was looking for.

"Aha!" She yelled, holding up a bright pink dildo. She hit the button on it and it started to spin and light up.

"Is that a dildo or a toy you buy at the circus?" Adalyn asked behind me.

"Oh my God, I could have gone a lifetime without knowing my sister owned any of this crap. I can't believe this," Ian muttered.

"Screw you, Chad. This is the newest model of Gerard. You can keep the old one!"

"Is that used?" I heard Blondie ask loudly in a disgusted voice.

"Just order a new one online you freaking weirdo!" I yelled at Stacy. I knew she wouldn't actually use it; she was just trying to make a point. But still...we're close, but not *that* close.

Chad pushed past me, but Stacy jumped onto my bed and ran across it standing up before jumping down to dart out of the room. She ran screaming down the hallway, yelling, "No! You can't have him!"

Everyone chased after them, except me, who took a second to lock the cabinet back up. I only locked it because of Stacy, anyway. She had a tendency to do this kind of dumb shit all the time.

When I made it back to the living room, I saw everyone forming a semicircle around Stacy, with Chad a little in front, and she was pointing the dildo at them like it was a switchblade or something. Everyone was stifling a laugh, even Chad. Well, except Blondie. *Shock.*

Chad and Stacy stood there at a standoff, until Blondie huffed and broke the silence. "That's it, I'm out of here. Your friends are batshit crazy."

I slapped my forehead with the palm of my hand. She couldn't just leave quietly? What started out as Stacy being ridiculous and trying to lighten the tension was going to turn into a violent altercation. Stacy couldn't look past someone insulting her friends, and everyone knew it, and we all instinctively took a step backwards.

"Are you coming?" Blondie turned and asked Joe when she reached the door.

She actually thought he'd go with her after she just called us all crazy? I mean, we were, especially Stacy, but still…

"I knew you were too good to be true," Blondie said, continuing to dig her grave. "When you finally decide to ditch these losers, come find me."

Before she could turn around, Gerard two-point-oh was flying across the room, directly at her head. A piercing cry rang out as the head of the dildo hit her square in the eye, and she dropped her bag, throwing her hands up to her face.

When she lowered her hand, you could already see the swelling that was starting around her eye. She was going to have a shiner.

Who knew dildos made such good weapons?

"You crazy bitch!" Blondie yelled, lunging at Stacy. Joe gripped Blondie from behind, wrapping his arms around her, and Chad did the same with Stacy. Blondie was fighting so hard that Joe finally let go. I assumed just from fear of hurting her, not because he couldn't hold her. I was a little sad, because watching the way his arms would flex while he held her back was deliciously entrancing. It made me tempted to take a swing at Stacy just so I could feel those strong arms restraining me instead.

"I'm pressing charges! That's assault!"

Blondie's threat had the opposite of it's intended effect on Stacy. Instead of Stacy feeling threatened, she started laughing. "Are you serious? You realize what Joe and Chad do for a living, right?"

Blondie looked between both men, expecting them to speak up on her behalf. When Chad did nothing, she glared daggers at Joe. He didn't look the least bit phased, and he just gave her a one shoulder shrug and said, "I didn't see anything."

Blondie snatched up her purse and when her hand was on the door handle I yelled out, "Thanks for coming by Darby!"

"It's Darcy!" She yelled, but I just waved at her dismissively, then she slammed the door behind her.

CHAPTER 5
JOE

I stuck behind after everyone left to help Carrie clean up her apartment. I felt bad for bringing that crazy woman to dinner. Lesson learned, though - next time I bring a date around Stacy, provide a disclaimer regarding flying dildos.

I could tell Carrie wanted me to leave and was too polite to insist, but we needed to talk. This avoiding each other nonsense was getting out of hand. For a second when I first got there with Darcy, I could have sworn she seemed a little jealous, but that could have just been me reading into things. Or if I was being entirely honest, more like wishful thinking.

It's not like I'd been living like a monk since meeting Carrie, but I was coincidentally having the longest dry spell of my adult life. I also spent a lot of time trying to convince myself that it was just that...a coincidence. That it had absolutely nothing to do with the tiny woman who all but tossed my world upside down over one stupid kiss.

I didn't know if it was her obvious lack of interest in me, or the lingering effects of that one kiss, but something about her just wouldn't let go of me. The few times I'd trying being with a woman since meeting Carrie, it had been so much of a struggle to not let her face pop into my mind that I had to feign illness or come up with other equally lame excuses. I couldn't have rumors spreading that I had issues with ED, but it was becoming clear that maintaining an erection was pretty damn difficult to do without letting my mind relive what it felt like to have her in my arms while our tongues danced. Not only did it feel creepy to picture her when I was with someone else, but it was disrespectful to the woman in my bed, so I'd been spending a lot of time with my right hand.

I knew my reputation with women. I didn't do commitment or relationships, and the women I hooked up with knew the score, but I always treated them with the respect they deserved. They were human beings, not just holes for me to stick my dick into. I knew my reputation eluded to me being some playboy or manslut, which wasn't entirely off base, but I was never the kind to love 'em and leave 'em. As long as they knew it wasn't going any further than sex, if they wanted a little cuddle after, I was down.

Truthfully, I hated being alone. Not alone, as in I needed a significant other, but just alone in general. It was the reason my house was always full of people, and why I never turned down an opportunity to gain a friend. Maybe that made me sad or desperate in some people's eyes, but that's only because they didn't know the reasons why I hated the silence.

Carrie and I washed dishes in silence, and it was both incredibly weird and surprisingly comfortable. We moved in a rhythm that would indicate we'd done been in that very spot hundreds of times before, but the quiet surrounding us made it glaringly obvious that there was an elephant that we'd yet to address.

Once her apartment was once again tidy and spotless, I stood near the door with my hands shoved awkwardly in my pockets. I didn't want to leave, I wanted to talk to her, get to know her. But if she felt the same way, she hid it well. If I had to take a stab at what she was feeling in that moment as we stood awkwardly by her door, I'd have to say she felt more like stabbing herself in the eye with an ink pen than spend any more time with me. Couldn't say it was entirely her fault she didn't have a high opinion of me, after the way I'd reacted to her and then shown up with an uninvited guest. No matter the reason, I wasn't going to give up easily.

"Listen, I wanted to-" I said at the same time Carrie said "Well, thanks for helping-" and we laughed nervously, doing the whole "you go first" bit a few times. Finally, I just took the plunge.

"I'm really sorry about Darcy. I should have known better than to bring a girl around that hadn't met any of my friends, especially Stacy. I didn't know she would behave that way." It was half an apology. I didn't believe for one second that she didn't know the real reason I'd

brought a date without telling anyone, and I half expected her to call me out on it.

She didn't, though. She just narrowed her eyes at
me, crossing her arms, and I took her response as my cue
to leave.

"Can I ask you a question?" Carrie asked me when
my hand touched the door handle, and I tried to ignore
the relief I felt, knowing I didn't have to leave just yet.

"Anything," I responded honestly.

"Why, exactly, did you bring her?"

*Well, shit. She wasn't going to let me off easy after
all.*

"I, uh…"

Carrie's cell phone started ringing, saving me mo-
mentarily. She ignored it and waited a few rings, as if she
expected me to answer her still. When I didn't speak up,
she sighed and walked over to her phone.

I didn't want her to feel like I was eavesdropping,
so I strolled around her living area, casually taking in
her apartment. Things had been so crazy all night that I
hadn't really taken the time to notice just how...empty
it felt. A few framed photos of her with Ian, Stacy and
Adalyn were all that adorned her mantle. No artwork or
shelves hung on her walls, and minimal furniture was
placed throughout the room.

I had hoped to learn a little about her by observing
her living space, and even though her apartment seemed

to be lacking, it also felt like that in itself was a huge clue. Just one more aspect of this woman that confused the hell out of me.

"Shit," Carrie muttered under her breath. I turned to see she'd ended her call, her hands deep in her hair, pulling hard from the roots. "Shit!"

"What? What's wrong?" I asked, running to her, afraid something bad had happened. Was it Ian? Stacy? Everyone had just left. Had there been a wreck? Carrie stayed silent, her eyes frantic, and the longer it took for her to answer me, the more nervous I became. "Carrie?" I asked her name like a question, and she finally seemed to snap out of her trance, and she startled, like she was surprised to see me.

"What? Oh, I'm sorry. No, everything's fine. I mean, it's not fine. Nothing is fine. This is a disaster. But it doesn't concern you, so no need to be worried." She was rambling, and I was holding her hands in mine, and she either didn't notice or didn't mind, so I didn't let go. "Thank you for helping me clean up and stuff tonight, I really appreciate it. But I've got a work emergency to deal with, so if you don't mind…"

"Let me help," I blurted out, not sure where that came from. Carrie smiled softly at me with an expression I couldn't read.

"You really are sweet, Joe. I see why Stacy and you are so close. Listen, I owe you an apology." Her mood shifted so fast it almost gave me whiplash.

"For what?"

"For lying to you."

I hadn't really talked to her, well, at all since we'd met. We'd had a few little tiffs in the beginning, but it was all cordial if we happened to cross paths nowadays, so I wasn't sure what she could be alluding to.

"I lied about the kiss. About not remembering."

I fought the urge to fist pump the air, my ego doing a little happy dance inwardly. I *knew* I wasn't fucking forgettable.

"It's dumb, I don't even know why I lied. I guess I thought maybe pretending it didn't happen would make things less awkward, but I think it just made it worse. For me, anyway. I don't normally get drunk and make out with random strangers, but I also don't like having to explain my actions. I guess I figured it was easier to go with denial than the truth."

"I'm not a random stranger." I wasn't sure why that was the point I wanted to make, but it was the first thing that slipped out of my mouth. Carrie smiled coyly at me, looking down and finally realizing our hands were en-twined.

"You aren't now, but you pretty much were then. I had just met you, and we barely said ten words to each other. You may as well have been any guy in the bar at that point."

Well, *shit*, that stung. I hoped she didn't mean it the way I took it, but it really sounded like she was saying that kiss had absolutely nothing to do with me. That if I hadn't been there, it would have happened with the closest set of lips. Meaning it meant nothing to her, and the fact that she could so easily pretend it didn't happen, meant she didn't feel anything either.

I was such an idiot. There was no denying I had developed a small thing for her since that night. Okay fine, much more than a small thing, which I held out hope would gradually diminish with the glaring realization that she didn't at all feel the same way. It wasn't working, despite my best efforts to move on, and hearing that I once again maybe had a chance to relive that moment sparked my attraction to her even more.

For one dumbass second I considered reliving that kiss right then, but when she released my hands and gave me a friendly smile, she made it perfectly clear that it didn't matter anymore what I did.

I was clearly in the friend zone. That had never happened to me, but I could recognize it all the same. And dammit, I didn't like it.

I took Carrie in for a second, looking at her hair that was wacky from tugging at it. Her shirt had a small stain over her left breast, probably from when she was cooking. Her clothes were slightly rumpled, and she didn't have a stitch of makeup on. She was nothing like the girls I usually went for. It was obvious she didn't make herself into something just to impress others, and that just added to her appeal. No, she wouldn't be walking down any runways in her disheveled state, but a naked Sports Illustrated model could walk up and snap their fingers in my face and I still wouldn't be able to look away from Carrie.

I didn't know at what point I took the pathetic turn from attraction into infatuation, but I was delusional enough to believe that my interest in her was based on looks alone. I didn't have to work to get laid, and I wasn't the type that set out to conquer. I didn't chase women, because the women who were okay with just hooking up and not getting serious didn't need to be chased.

Carrie wasn't the hooking up type. At least, based on everything I'd heard and seen, I didn't think she was. And somewhere deep down, since that first night, I think I always knew what I was getting myself into. I wasn't being lured in her direction just because it was a challenge. I genuinely liked her personality. She was feisty, honest and loyal.

It might be a mistake, and it may end badly, but I was going to find a way to get her to let me in. If nothing other than friendship came of it, so be it, but I knew she was worth the effort.

I realized I had been staring, unmoving and not speaking, for quite some time. So I cleared my throat and started towards the door.

"Thank you for telling me. I guess I don't need to follow through with my plan," I said to her as she held the door open for me from behind.

"Oh? What plan?" She let go of the door and crossed her arms, looking at me curiously. I shrugged and took a small step towards her, closing the distance between us.

"I was going to *make* you remember." Her eyebrows shot up, her arms falling to her sides. She took in a sharp breath and held it as I took one more step, putting us nose to nose.

"How?" She breathed out, her breath fanning my face. She smelled like mint and red wine, and fuck, I wanted a taste.

"Like this," I said as I gripped the nape of her neck with one hand, pulling her mouth to mine, while my other hand gripped her hip.

She stilled at first, but quickly melted into me. I had to bend down while she stood on her tippy toes to meet me, so I slid my hands down to her thighs and tugged. She came easily, wrapping her legs around my waist. I kicked the door closed behind me, then spun around, pushing her up against it.

The kiss started off hard and desperate, but as soon as I had her secure in my arms and felt her returning my kiss, I slowed my movements. She caught on quickly and let me take the lead, her legs tightening around my waist as my hand moved from her thigh and up her torso until I was cupping her tit in my hand.

When we pulled apart, panting and gasping for air, I pressed my forehead to hers. I was shaking with need, and resisting the urge to carry her to her bedroom and fuck her right then was the hardest thing I'd ever done.

"What are you doing to me, Carrie?" My voice came out sounding weak and pained, and I should have been embarrassed about that, but it was how I felt around her. Weak, for not being able to fight whatever was drawing me to her. And pained, from not being able to have her like I want. I'd never been one to hide away my emotions, I wasn't afraid of being vulnerable, but I'd never been vulnerable with a woman. It scared the shit out of me.

She didn't answer me, instead pressing a soft kiss on my jaw, slow and sensual. As she continued her tender kisses along my jaw line, down my neck and back up to my mouth, I groaned loudly. She was testing my willpower, and if she didn't stop soon, I wasn't going to even bother trying to hold back anymore.

"What is it about you?" I asked aloud, more of a rhetorical question than anything. "You're nothing like the women I'm usually attracted to. But I can't quit thinking about you."

Carrie's mouth froze on my neck, her whole body tensing up. I didn't know what I'd said or done to ruin the moment, but it was clear it was over. She was shutting down, and when she pulled back and looked at me, I could have sworn I saw her blinking back tears.

She relaxed her legs and I let her place them on the floor, and I took a step back. I wasn't going to force her, and everything about her was screaming for me to give her space.

"I'm sorry. I got caught up in the moment, please forgive me. Thank you for helping. It's time for you to go."

Her cold tone was businesslike as she held the door open, staring at the ground and refusing to make eye contact. She'd opened herself up to me for a moment, but her walls were firmly back in place. And it fucking hurt. I wanted to reach out to her, hold her, beg her to just tell me what had changed and let me fix it. In that moment with her, having her mouth on mine and feeling her in my arms, it just felt...right.

"Carrie..." I whispered, taking a step towards her, but her shoulders stiffened and curled inward slightly, like she was physically pulling into herself. So I left. I left without saying goodbye, because if my voice alone was hurting her, then I couldn't bring myself to speak any more.

The steps to my car were heavy with regret, and each time I moved farther away from her, it felt like I was walking through quicksand. I didn't regret kissing her, but I regretted how it all happened. I shouldn't have brought Darcy. I should have just been upfront with her about my attraction from the beginning, instead of just attacking her.

Now, more than ever, though, it was glaringly obvious that Carrie had no desire to be anything romantic with me. If friendship was all she would give me, then I would take it.

Even if the thought of never kissing her again made something in my chest physically ache.

CHAPTER 6
CARRIE

Kicking Joe out of my apartment the other night left me with what Stacy would call a "cliffy" for days. Cliffy, you ask? Stacy's female equivalent of blue balls - an amalgamation of the words "clit" and "stiffy". I was so worked up, and if he hadn't reminded me of why it was such a bad idea for us to be pursuing our baser urges, then I would have gone to bed with him.

Him saying I was nothing like the women he's usually attracted to was like having a bucket of ice water thrown on my libido. He probably thought he offended me somehow, but not falling into the category of Joe's usual conquests wasn't an insult. I didn't *want* to be like the other women he'd slept with, and I was happy with who I was.

His rhetorical question served as a reminder that he wasn't the only one going out of his comfort zone. I was attracted to Joe, sure, but it was more than just physical. I liked his personality, his sense of humor and his confidence. I could see myself spending time with him, fully clothed, and actually enjoying it. That meant he needed to be placed firmly in the friend-zone, because I did not sleep with people who had the potential to mean more to me than casual sex.

It was one of my rules. I didn't have many, but they were important. I had a heart, and when I chose to let someone in then I cared deeply for them, and sex wasn't just physical for me if I really knew the person. I couldn't afford to get attached, which is why any hookup I participated in had to be with someone that I felt zero chemistry with. A girl can only get her heart broken so many times before she breaks beyond repair, and it would be over my dead body before I'd give another man a chance to finally destroy me completely.

It didn't matter if they said they were looking to settle down. They could fancy up their resume however they wanted and spew empty promises all night long, but it wouldn't change a damn thing. Men are controlled by their dicks, as much as they want to think that's not the case, and fidelity is a frivolous to the vast majority of people. Some of them might have higher morals, and some may have enough willpower to say no for a while, but if the right temptation comes along then even the noblest of men are capable of falling weak to their knees.

All behold the mighty powers of the vagina.

Too bad my lady parts were broken.

Plus, I had bigger things to worry about beyond the fleeting moments of physical satisfaction. That phone call had been from Reed, the owner of Grind, and the person I was currently trying to work out a business agreement with.

My studio had been working for months on the routines, and I'd sent away all my dancers for a much needed break when Reed had told me the trial performance had been pushed up too much sooner than anticipated. Apparently a potential investor had some kind of an emergency and couldn't make it for the original date, and said investor must have been really damn important, because they were suddenly available and I had to snap my fingers and make my dancers all magically appear by this weekend.

I wasn't worried about their ability to perform; I was worried about getting them all back in time. Some of them were halfway across the world visiting family, and getting sooner flights would cost a fortune. So far everyone was trying to move heaven and earth to get back here, and I could ask Ian to call in some favors if necessary, but I was too stubborn to ask for help unless I absolutely had to.

So I tried not to stress too much, hoping that by the power of wishful thinking, everything would just work itself out. 'Coz you know, my luck was always so freaking phenomenal.

I was meeting Reed at Grind to do a walkthrough of what was to happen during the performance, and as I pulled up to the club there was a police cruiser parked out front. It was the middle of the day and the club wasn't open to the public, so I assumed everything was fine. I laughed at myself for the little twinge of anticipation that came with the possibility that it could be Joe inside.

I rang the bell since the doors were locked, calling myself a few choice names under my breath while I waited, and a few minutes later an extremely beautiful woman answered the door. She gave me a broad, friendly smile that seemed genuine enough to have me immediately liking her. Which was rare for me, because I tend to be pretty cynical about people.

She introduced herself as Lacy, one of the managers of the club, and explained that she was in charge of the bars and their staffing. Considering Grind had three separate bars inside it's walls, I figured that was a pretty challenging job. Lacy had the kind of looks that would suit her more for a ditzy bartender position, but she seemed competent enough and Reed only hired the best of the best, so I trusted she was good at what she did.

I'd been inside the club many times, but never when it was empty and quiet. It was weird and kind of eerie. I took a seat at the bar, per Lacy's instructions, waited for Reed to finish up in a meeting.

"Well, well. Fancy seeing you here," a male voice rang out behind me. I clenched my fists and pasted on a smile before turning to face him.

"Joe," I replied cordially. I was in no frame of mind to dance around whatever game we'd been playing at since we met, and I needed to stay focused for my meeting with Reed.

Joe quirked an eyebrow at me and opened his mouth to reply, but Lacy interrupted him.

"There's my sexy policeman. Get everything you need?"

Joe cleared his throat nervously, stealing a glance at me, as Lacy ran a seductive finger down his chest. Just like that my opinion of her was flushed down the crapper, and the jealousy I felt while watching her slutty hands pawing at him had absolutely nothing to do with it.

Lacy was seemingly unaware at how uncomfortable Joe was, but it was clear as day to me. The worst part was knowing I was the reason for his discomfort. If I weren't there, he'd probably be eating up her attention and pawing her right back. I suddenly felt like I was cock-blocking him, which had me feeling equal parts proud and pissed off. I started to get up and excuse myself, leave them to flirt without an audience, but the thought of them flirting made jealousy rear it's stupid, very much unwanted head.

I had no right to be jealous, but that didn't stop the green eyed monster from possessing me. New Carrie would have ignored it, made the effort to put aside her pride and not intervene. But the green eyed monster had devoured New Carrie whole when Lacy very un-secretively cupped Joe's ass and gave it a good squeeze. To hell with being the bigger person. I'd be damned if I was going to stand by and let her touch my man.

What the hell? *My man?*

Whatever. Pushing that Freudian slip aside, I leapt to my feet and rushed over to where they were standing. I watched Joe's eyes widen a fraction when he saw me literally storming in their direction. I couldn't even tell you what the hell I was doing, and I knew I was going to regret it. But dammit, when her hand wandered from his ass towards the front of his pants...

"Hey sweetie," I said sweetly, slipping my arm through his and pressing my side against him affection-ately. I wanted to kick her in her shin or slap her hand away from him, but somehow I managed to just lay my head on his shoulder and wait for her reaction. Lacy slowly pulled her hand away from Joe, looking at me like I had three heads. Guess I needed to make my inten-tions a little more obvious. "Oh, you're *that* Lacy. I don't know how I didn't put two and two together. I'm such a ditz sometimes."

I smacked my forehead with my palm. I was any-thing but a ditz, but Stacy had forced me to watch *Clue-less* so many times in our youth that I could summon up an airhead persona if need be. Joe must have caught on to what I was doing, because I felt his stiff body relax as I started casually running my fingertips through the hair at the nape of his neck. Or maybe he just liked having his hair played with. Whatever.

"Um, I didn't...I mean...how do you two..."

I bit down on my lip to stifle my laugh as I watched her stutter through her thoughts. She wanted to ask how we knew each other, and what I was to him, but she was afraid to come out and say it. I let her suffer a few more seconds, but was worried if I didn't speak first, then Joe would go and say something to ruin the little facade I was putting on, so I gave her a smile before spinning and putting my front completely flush to Joe's.

He wore his uniform well, and as I slid my hands up his chest and around his neck, I couldn't help but react naturally to the hard body I felt underneath. My fingers continued to toy with his hair before I gently pulled his head down towards mine. His knowing smirk fell from his face when it registered what I was about to do, but instead of resisting like I feared he might, he dove right in.

As soon as his lips touched mine, all the control I had over our situation slipped away. I was no longer trying to scare off Lacy, or ruin Joe's chances of getting laid. I wasn't doing anything, except standing there being helplessly devoured, unable to do anything but savor what was hands down the most passionate kiss I'd ever had.

It wasn't a kiss stemmed from drunken impulsivity, meant to piss off my ex. It wasn't a kiss of lust, though I could feel his desire for me through his extremely well fitted slacks. No, that kiss contained more than I would ever be able to comprehend. I felt my chest expanding as I breathed him in. Felt my walls crumbling when his tongue gently massaged mine. The darkness of my past faded away as his large hand splayed across my lower back, pulling me closer to him.

What started out as an immature ploy to keep another woman away from someone I wouldn't even let myself have turned into a moment that threatened to wreck me. Our lips moved slowly and sensually, his hold on me tender and careful. I'd been denying him at every turn, and I realized a large part of me expected him to push me away and call me out on my bullshit. He had every right to seize the opportunity to humiliate me or get even for how I'd treated him, but he didn't.

He kissed me like we were the only ones in the room. Like I was the only one that mattered. It felt too real, too wonderful. There was a safety in his arms that I'd never felt before, and I was suddenly hit with a wave of emotion. When I felt tears start to prick at the corners of my eyes, I forced myself to pull back. I tried to immediately look away, not wanting him to see my reaction to him, but he cupped my face in his palms and looked straight into my eyes, swiping away a traitorous tear I hadn't been able to hold back with the pad of his thumb.

I was mortified at my emotional response, and a normal man would have been equally mortified to see a woman they weren't even dating cry just from a kiss. I waited for him to run away, or look at me like I was nuts, but he did neither. He searched my eyes, and reality hit me like a punch to the gut. He wasn't freaked out by my tears, he didn't even seem phased, like he already knew the reason. I felt vulnerable and exposed as he stared at me.

I'd never felt longing before, but that had to be what I was feeling right then. An intense longing for him to hold me close to his chest with his strong arms wrapped tightly around me every day. To be thinking things that included the notion of a future was so beyond my comprehension it was laughable, but even with no explanation for it, I knew he could always provide me that feeling of safety. From the pain, from the past, and from myself.

Someone clearing their throat broke our trance, and I took a shaky step backwards, Joe's hands falling from my face. I looked up to see Reed smirking at me, and a very confused Lacy next to her. There was no malice mixed in with her confusion, which was a relief. I hadn't thought about making an enemy when I so stupidly caused this spectacle. The last thing I needed was to piss off Reed right before the big show.

I could tell my face was flushed, and it took every damn ounce of pride left in me to keep from hanging my head in shame. It was unprofessional and a little brazen of me to behave that way when I was waiting for a business meeting, but Reed didn't seem all too upset about it, so I wasn't going to apologize unnecessarily.

"This isn't over," Joe whispered into my ear, causing goose bumps to rise all over my body. He placed a chaste kiss on my cheek before waving goodbye to Reed, and I took a second to compose myself by pretending to smooth out my skirt and blouse. When I looked back up to Reed, she was covering her mouth with her hand and failing to stifle a laugh, which made me laugh.

"Shut up," I teased her. "Let's get this show on the road."

JOE

"What?" I asked Stacy, who was staring at me from the other side of the breakfast bar in her house. I'd texted Carrie three times after that damn kiss. I was tempted to cuff myself to my own bed to keep from tracking her down and kissing her again. My need to taste her only grew more and more each time we kissed, and it didn't take a genius to figure out it was fucking with my head.

Since I had no clue what was going on with myself, I sought out Stacy's wisdom, which was a mistake. She was worse at relationships than I was, even though she'd somehow managed to find happiness with my best friend, Chad. That was probably because he was as dysfunctional as her, and I was happy for them and all, but that meant the two people I could turn to for advice would have absolutely none to give me.

Not advice worth taking, anyway. Yet, there I was, sitting there saying absolutely nothing. Too chicken shit to admit I needed help, and honestly, a little afraid Stacy was going to give me a ton of shit over this.

"What's going on between you and Carrie?" She asked, raising her eyebrows when I choked on my beer.

"Nothing," I said between coughs. Had Carrie talked to her? Did she know what Carrie was feeling? Obviously not, or she wouldn't be asking me. Or maybe she just wanted my side of things. Or maybe I was over-analyzing everything like a twelve-year-old girl. "Why would you think that?"

"Because I'm not an idiot. You guys avoid each other most of the time, and then when I manage to get you both in the same place, you won't even look at each other. You can cut the sexual tension with a knife, so cut the crap and tell me what's going on."

"Isn't this the kind of girly bullshit conversation you should be having with her, and not me?" I wasn't going to elaborate, but the look Stacy was giving me told me that if I didn't, she would come to her own conclusion, which would be way different from the truth. I came here to get information, not give it, but if I had to give something up to get answers from her, then I was willing to relent. Yeah, I was getting pretty pathetic at that point.

"Okay fine, I'm attracted to her, and I'm pretty sure she's attracted to me. It's not like I'm going to do anything about it, she's your best friend and I don't do relationships. Something tells me that a quick hookup with her would not bode well for any of us. She's so opposite of you. I don't know how you guys are friends. She's just so...confusing." Stacy snorted, and took a drink of the coffee she was drinking out of her "Blow Me, I'm Hot" mug.

"I know it makes me sound like a dick, but when I first met her I thought she was kind of a frigid bitch. She came across as kind of stuck up, but then she surprised the shit out of me. Every time I think I have her pegged, she does something completely out of left field." Another snort. "She's not even my type. At all. So I'm not even sure why I can't get her out of my head. I mean, do you hear me right now? Talking and thinking like a little bitch? I've never given a shit what a woman was thinking about. I never tried to figure someone out. I mean, what the hell?" An even louder snort.

"You okay over there, Stace? Got something stuck in your nose?" Stacy didn't answer, just shrugged and gave me a knowing smile. "Apparently you know something I don't, and I'm sorry if I sound like a prick, but I'm just being honest. She's confusing the hell out of me, so if you could give me a little insight I would appreciate it. She's just so...tightly wound." Snort.

"Okay, that's getting annoying. If you're just going to keep making noises at me and not contribute to the conversation, then I'm heading out." Stacy eyed me over her coffee mug, like it was some big decision whether or not she was going to talk about Carrie. I had to admit, her being so secretive about Carrie made me even more curious.

"Sometimes...sometimes looks can be deceiving, Joe. Especially with Carrie."

"That's it? You sat there looking like you were about to dump some big secret on me, and you give me a cliché saying? What the hell does that even mean?" My voice was a little too loud and a little too annoyed, but Stacy didn't seem affected in the least as she walked over to the sink and rinsed out her mug. She turned back to face me and leaned back on the counter, her palms flat behind her on the edge of the sink. Her eyes narrowed, like she was trying to be intimidating, but she was still wearing that damn smirk.

"All I'm saying is, everyone has layers. Carrie just... she has more than most. You do what you want, you're an adult and just because you and I are friends doesn't mean you have to spend time with Carrie. If you want to fuck her, fuck her. You want to date her, you have my blessing. Because despite your whorish ways, I know you're a good guy and wouldn't promise her something you can't give. But hear me when I say this - you better watch yourself." Stacy delivered that last line with a finger jammed into my chest, before walking out of the room.

I followed her out of the kitchen and called out to her when she was halfway down the hall. Apparently she was done visiting with me. "I'm not even sure what the hell is going on, and I'm not going to screw up the dynamics between so many people just to get her naked. You don't have to worry about me breaking her heart or something." Stacy turned back to face me and laughed, delivering one last line before disappearing into her bedroom.

"I was more worried about her breaking yours."

CHAPTER 7
JOE

I checked my phone for the hundredth time, and yeah, each time I had text messages or missed calls. Never from the person I wanted it to be. I'd turned into a damn stalker since Carrie acted like a jealous girlfriend and kissed me at Grind.

I'd never hooked up with Lacy, she was just a relentless flirt. But seeing Carrie get jealous was such a turn on, there was no way in hell I was going to explain that to her. When she stalked over to me I couldn't get a read on her expression, but once I figured out her game I half expected her to get all bitchy and catty. I never thought she'd lay claim to me and kiss me like that.

Damn, that kiss. All of her kisses. My hand did nothing to relieve the tension from the feeling of her tight body up against mine. I wanted more. *Needed* more of her. How the hell some plain, tiny little enigma of a woman managed to get me wrapped around her damn finger without even putting out…

Clearly, I was broken. My head. My dick. Nothing worked anymore. She consumed my every thought, and as tempting as it had been to just get blasted and try to forget her while buried inside someone else, I couldn't do it. Furthermore, I didn't *want* to do it. She had me by the balls, metaphorically anyway. And dammit, I wanted her to have them literally, too.

I liked to think of myself as a considerate person, both in the bed and out of it. I gave pleasure just as well as I took it, but I'd never felt the need to exert power over a woman. Maybe that was because they so willingly gave the power to me, so there was nothing to demand.

Carrie though...she was pulling out every alpha male, caveman instinct I didn't even know I had inside of me. The desire to go to her, throw her over my shoulder and just tie her to my bed so she couldn't keep running from me was getting out of control. She was so damn stubborn, but I knew she wanted me. If she would just give me half a chance to show her how great we could be together, I'd make sure she never regretted it.

I hadn't the first clue how to be a boyfriend, but I'd figure it out. Carrie deserved romance. She deserved to be worshipped. I had heard the stories of how she treated Adalyn in the beginning, and Stacy had told me enough to know that Carrie wasn't perfect. But neither am I, and even without knowing her reasons for being so closed off, I knew I could help her with them. More so, I *wanted* to be the one who helped her.

"What the fuck, man?"

I looked up at Dorian and glared. "Language." I

didn't really care if the kids cussed, but I felt obligated to at least put up the pretense of trying to be a good influence.

Dorian laughed and threw the basketball at me, hard enough that I almost didn't catch it, because my head was so damn distracted with thoughts of Carrie. I shook my head, trying to focus on the game, but it was useless. The kids ribbed me the entire time, and I couldn't even defend myself because I really was off my game.

I felt horrible because I'd missed a few weekends at the community center where I normally came to hang out every Saturday. That place was like a second home to me, and I felt like a big brother to these kids, and going so long without visiting made me feel like crap.

After my parents died, the community center was the only place I felt safe. Most of the staff was still there, but of course the kids were different, but I felt it was my duty to give back what was given to me.

I finally managed to get my head back in the game, but it didn't stay there for long.

"Yo, Miss D!" Tye, another one of the kids I visited frequently, yelled out. I squinted in the bright sun and saw a female figure standing outside of the tall chain link fence that surrounded the basketball court.

The kids talked about "Miss D" all the time, but she'd never been there at the same time as me so we'd never met. She was wildly popular with the kids and they spoke very highly of her, and I kept hoping we'd run into one another. Looked like I was going to get my chance to thank her personally for volunteering her own time at the center.

Tye and Dorian jogged over to her, and I tried to shade my eyes with my hand, but between the glaring sun and the distance I still couldn't make out her features. I couldn't hear what they were saying, but the outlines of their bodies were animated enough to make it possible to understand the conversation. The boys were gesturing for her to join us, and she shook her head at first, but then she threw her head back and looked to the sky. I couldn't help but laugh. Those boys were nothing if not convincing. They could talk their way out of or into anything.

The mysterious Miss D made her way back with the boys, and I followed her steps as they made their way towards me. Something about her seemed so familiar. My eyes were starting to water from squinting in the sunlight, so I couldn't see her face, but her petite and curvy frame had my lower parts reacting nicely. It was the first time since the last time I saw Carrie that I felt even slightly aroused by another woman.

I dribbled in place, trying to make it look like I was doing something other than staring while she stopped to talk to several kids along the way. Her back was to me, and she was finally in a position where the sun was blocked and I could get a nice view of her.

Why did her ass look familiar? That seemed like an odd thing to recognize. Maybe she was someone I'd hooked up with in the past? *Shit, that would make things complicated.* The last thing I wanted was to drag my personal life into my work at the community center.

Dread crept in when I considered the ramifications of a possible rift with another volunteer. There was only a handful of women I'd ever slept with that turned out to be a problem afterward. Ones that said they understood there was no promise of a future, but had hoped to be 'the one' to change me, and then went a little nutso when that didn't turn out to be the case. It would be some seriously shitty luck if this woman turned out to be one of those.

None of those worries had caused my physical reaction to her to diminish. The closer she got, the more I could make out her figure. She was wearing short spandex running shorts with a tight fitting racerback tank, and there couldn't have been an ounce of fat on her. Her legs and arms were toned, making her slim body look healthy and not sickly like some women. Her stomach was completely flat, which made her beautifully large chest stick out prominently.

I turned away from her, feeling a semi coming on, which would have been bad news for me since I was wearing athletic shorts. Last thing I needed was having the kids teasing me for months about getting an erection. They would have a field day with that shit.

Once I went back to shooting hoops and stopped ogling strange women like some kind of creepy stalker my thoughts drifted back to Carrie. From out of nowhere a wave of guilt rushed over me. *What the fuck?* Why the hell did feeling attracted to someone all of a sudden feel like I was somehow doing something wrong? Like some sort of betrayal to Carrie? We hadn't even been on a date, so I shouldn't feel any kind of loyalty towards her. She was probably off fucking a different guy every day for all I knew.

Dammit, that was an asshole thing to assume. Carrie didn't give me any reason to believe she ran around town spreading her legs, and to assume she did wouldn't make me feel any better anyway. As a matter of fact, it had quite the opposite effect. Thinking of Carrie letting another man touch her made me want to forget where I was and all about my momentary attraction to this random woman so I could run to Carrie and claim her as mine.

And I would, if I wasn't scared shitless of being rejected again. Yeah, that's right, I wasn't too proud to admit I was scared. There was a limit to how many times my ego could withstand that kind of rejection. So I'd decided I wasn't going to try for another shot until I had a plan. A sure fire way to get her to into my bed, and not just for one night.

Just when I started picturing Carrie in my bed, her hair splayed out over my pillow, her back arching as she calls out my name...she appeared in front of me. Like I'd conjured her up using just my imagination. Or maybe I was just hallucinating. Whatever cruel joke my brain was playing on my eyes was so believable that I had to consider the possibility that I'd actually lost my damn mind over this woman.

Tye and Dorian were standing next to Miss D, now directly in front of me, and I swear she could have been Carrie's doppelganger. Either that, or my constant obsessing over her so badly had me picturing her face on all women, like those cartoons where the dog is so hungry that everything turns into a steak.

"Hey, Officer J, this is Miss D. The lady we've been telling you about."

I stepped towards her, my hand outstretched, and in closing that small distance it was like the fog cleared and my vision focused. I blinked, trying to compose myself and refrain from punching myself in the face for being such an idiot. Because damn it all to hell - the woman whose hand I was about to shake really *was* Carrie. I was stunned, which really was a gross understatement. She stood there giving me the sexiest smile while I was frozen in place with my mouth gaping open.

"What...how...*you?*" I was well aware that I sounded like a blubbering jackass, but I couldn't believe it.

Literally just couldn't wrap my head around the fact that Miss D was Carrie. Carrie was Miss D. For almost a year I'd been hearing stories about the wonderful Miss D. She was there almost as much, if not more, than I was. She'd started an outreach program in the community where the kids gathered for dance lessons and would put on an annual show. The first one was last month, but I didn't remember seeing her there.

"Wow. I'm impressed." I hadn't meant for it to come out patronizing, but I could tell right away that that's how she took it. She flipped some sort of internal switch, and her sexy smile turned into a tight-lipped grimace, her eyes narrowing as she crossed her arms. *Shit*, defensive Carrie was a pain in my ass.

"How little you must think of me if finding out I spend time here is such a shock to you." She turned her scowl to the boys and the group flinched. Every single one of them was almost twice her size and could probably hold up well in a fight against even myself, but they all cowered down to her. "Boys, give us a minute," she said sternly. They nodded and backed away, and Carrie missed it, but I didn't. I saw the look in their eyes. Those boys admired her. She definitely had their respect.

"You know I didn't mean it like that," I started as soon as the boys were out of earshot. "You have to admit it's a little shocking that we spend so much time here, but have never met. Did you already know who I was?"

"No, they call you J. And I'm sorry, I didn't mean to get defensive. It's a habit I'm trying to break." Her shoulders relaxed and she looked away, distracted or avoiding my gaze, I wasn't sure which. So I took the opportunity to look her over. Her long hair was in a messy, high ponytail and as usual, she wore no makeup. A light sheen of sweat glistened on her chest, drawing my attention to her wonderfully perky tits. After taking a few seconds to give them the admiration they deserved, I moved on to inspect the rest of her.

She looked so much younger for some reason. Her clothes showed off her size, and she looked small and frail. I knew she wasn't - she could probably kick my ass if she set her mind to it. That was probably one of the reasons why she tended to get defensive. I'd bet anything that her whole life people treated her like an incapable child because of how sweet and helpless she looked. I wanted to know if I was right. I wanted to know about her childhood and what her life was like growing up, what turned her into the person she is today. If only I could get her to open up to me...

"Well, listen guys, I really can't stay. Just wanted to say hi while I was out and about." She gave me a tight, forced smile. "Good seeing you."

I watched as the kids waved as the distance between us grew, but I couldn't let her walk away. I knew she didn't want my company, but she was going to get it anyway.

"Hey, half-pint! Wait up!" I half expected her to take off sprinting away from me, but to my surprise she stopped and waited. "What are your plans today?"

"My studio is down the street. I was going to work on some choreography and stuff today. Why?" She eyed me suspiciously, but she knew damn well that I was going to be following her there.

"Oh good, I've always wanted to see a dance studio. Maybe you can give me some lessons." She rolled her eyes, but I stood my ground. "Lead the way, half-pint."

She groaned but started walking, giving in a little too easily, which made me a little nervous.

"So, I didn't really have to talk you into spending time with me...you got something evil planned for me?"

She laughed, and it was sweet and musical. I could see why she didn't do it often. Laugh, that is. It was a moment of pure, genuine vulnerability. If you weren't watching her closely, you might not catch it, but it was there. I missed the sound already.

"No, no evil plan. At least, not today, anyway." She winked at me, and that one little gesture made my pants grow tighter. My body just reacted to her, almost like it had been trained to recognize hers without thought. Never in my life had someone turned me on so badly without even trying. And she wasn't trying, that was for sure.

She never did anything intentionally to get attention, and I would be the first to admit that it was easy to overlook her at first. The way she dressed plainly so as to fade into the background made it obvious she didn't want to be the center of attention. It made sense why she was friends with Stacy. You couldn't go anywhere with Stacy without her commanding the room's attention be placed solely on her, and Carrie would never compete with her for that, so they made the perfect pair.

I'd always been drawn more to Stacy's type, and while I loved Stacy dearly, the more time I spent with Carrie the more I wondered what the appeal had ever been for me with those types of women. Overtly sexual, proudly showing off their bodies like the word 'modesty' was taboo to them. In the past, a woman who exuded sex in everything she did would be a huge turn on. Now, the thought of taking one of those women to bed made me feel...empty.

If I ever got Carrie in my bed, it would be just for me, a private show. Clearly a man would have to earn the right to see her naked, and that made what she had beneath her homely clothes seem like a hidden treasure. A well kept secret that would be all mine. Hypothetically, anyway.

My ego wanted to declare that it was inevitable that Carrie would end up naked beneath me, but the realistic part of my brain reminded me that there were absolutely no guarantees when it came to her. I never knew where

I stood from one minute to the next, and knowing if I would ever get to explore her hidden treasures still remained a mystery.

Which naturally only made me want it more.

Conversation was light and easy as we trekked to her studio, which turned out, was only a few minutes away from the center. Yet another piece of the Carrie puzzle that had been directly in front of my face for a ridiculous amount of time. Didn't matter now though, because having gained more valuable intel meant Carrie might be getting some surprise visits from me. I had the urge to rub my hands together and laugh evilly, knowing how easy it was to catch her off guard and get under her skin.

Her studio was part of an old brick building, sandwiched between an attorney and a vitamin store. I'd been down that street thousands of times, and knew it well, yet still never realized there was a dance studio taking up space in the building nestled in the historical division of the city.

It was much larger inside than it looked from outside, and I was fully impressed, which of course I let her know. She took the compliments in stride, blushing from time to time, but mostly beaming with pride. After giving me a quick tour, I followed her to the middle of a room that had mirrors as walls and a hardwood floor. The room was bare aside from a stereo system in the corner and a long metal bar that I couldn't help picturing her bent over while I plowed into her from behind.

"Alright, bud," Carrie said as she came to a halt. "You asked for a lesson, so let's get it started."

CHAPTER 8
CARRIE

Joe put his hand in mine, shocking the shit out of me. I was positive he was going to back out of the 'dance lesson', assuming it had just been a ploy to spend time with me. I didn't actually expect him to follow through with it, but there he was, his hand in mine, awaiting my instructions.

I cleared my throat and attempted to clear my head, trying to remember what the hell we were doing. Oh yeah, dance lesson.

"Okay, well, what kind of training have you had?" I tried to keep my tone professional, the way I would talk to a new student, trying to quell my nerves at the thought of having Joe so close to me.

"Uhhh, not much, unless you count grinding up on beautiful women at dance clubs." It was an appalling answer, but his sexy smile made it impossible to dwell on how much of a douchey response that was. I wanted to make a smart-ass remark about it, but in trying to keep with my professional persona, I managed to avoid doing so.

"Yeah, no, that doesn't count. So what would you like to learn?" There were so many different types of dance, and not knowing his skill level, it would be hard to determine where to start. Not that I seriously thought any real dancing would occur. Joe and I alone and in each other's arms was a recipe for disaster, and I wasn't sure if we would end up ruining this moment by trying to rip each other's throats out or rip each other's clothes off. I honestly couldn't tell you which one I'd prefer if I were forced to choose.

My breath caught in my throat when Joe reached out and tugged on my hand, pulling me flush against his chest. One big hand gripped my waist just above my hip, the heat of his touch singeing through my clothes and burning a memory into my skin. His other hand held my arm up in the air, palm to palm, in a stance similar to closed position. His erection pressing against my hip was distracting, and when he spoke, I could feel his warm breath on my hair and neck. His cheek so close to mine that he could probably tell I was blushing just from his nearness, the heat of all the blood rushing to my face hot enough to take the room temperature up a few degrees.

"Whatever kind of dance that gets you in my arms. That's the kind of dance I want to learn."

His words, his hard body, his manly scent - it was almost too much. Everything Joe did was too much and not enough. My core throbbed and my heart raced, and there was no mistaking the shiver that went through me. He must have taken my very obvious reaction to him as a permission of sorts, because his hand slipped down from my waist to very blatantly cup my ass. Which he then took the liberty of squeezing.

My palms started to sweat. I hadn't been this nervous around a guy since middle school. Joe was probably attracted to the kind of women who would revel in his sexy teasing. The kind that would flirt back, not break into a sweat and get stomach cramps just by standing near him.

It occurred to me that I may end up having to tackle the Joe issue with a more head-on approach. Like five years ago when I went bungee jumping to try and get over my fear of heights. The idea sounded ludicrous at the time when Stacy suggested it, and I was convinced she was trying to manipulate me into another one of her shenanigans. But research on the subject proved her to be correct, surprising as that was. So I went along with it, and funnily enough, I've been bungee jumping three more times since then.

Of course, I wasn't afraid of Joe, per se. More like I was afraid of the things he made me feel. Feelings I seemed to have no control over when it came to him. I wasn't anywhere near ready to face the feelings part of it, but I could make a better effort to get over the physical reactions.

I slipped out of his grasp and walked over to the sound system, grateful for the reprieve. I needed to get a grip on myself before I did something stupid and licked his beautiful face. After selecting a medium tempo song, I begrudgingly made my way back over to him.

Now or never, Care. Right?

Joe caught on quickly, soon taking over the lead, gliding us smoothly across the dance floor. My heartbeat was tripping over itself more than his feet were over the moves, and my nerves were making *me* look like the amateur. Images crept into my mind of him holding me in this exact way, only instead of being in my little studio, we would be on the dance floor at our wedding reception.

I'd never imagined myself getting married, it was a life meant for someone else. Someone who didn't have the baggage and emotional issues that I did. Half the time when I was around Joe I couldn't decide if I wanted to kiss him or smack him, so daydreaming about freaking marrying him made all the heat in my body turn to ice in my veins.

I jerked back suddenly, ignoring Joe's confused face, and mumbled some excuse about needing to get ready for my next class. I left out that the next class wasn't until the next day, because that was just semantics really. What was important was getting my head on straight, which meant getting away from Joe.

After all but pushing Joe out the door, I turned the music back on. Nothing took my mind off worries and stress better than dancing. I put my heart and soul into the moves, using every part of my body to express my conflicted emotions. Every other time in my life when I'd danced alone, putting every piece of myself into the music, it was cathartic and therapeutic. Even when my parents were fighting, when dad walked out on us, when mom was too drunk to give a shit...nothing ever came between me and dancing.

Only this time...this time it wasn't working. I couldn't shut off my brain, couldn't keep my anxiety over this Joe situation at bay long enough to lose myself in the dance. I turned the music up, hoping to drown out my thoughts, but by the end of the song I was slumped on the floor with tears streaming down my face.

No man had ever put so much effort into being near me, spend time with me and get to know me. No man had ever looked at me like Joe did. It was an intense look, and no matter where we were or who was around, his attentions didn't waver. At first it felt scrutinizing, but the more time I spent with him the clearer it became just how wrong I was about him.

He was different with me. I didn't know what that meant, exactly, but I wasn't blind to the way he treated me versus the way he treated everyone else. *Shit.* If I was able to tell the difference between his expressions enough to get a good read on him, then I was getting entirely too close. He was affecting me in ways I wasn't ready to face, but he was breaking me down, bit by bit, and pretty soon I wouldn't be able to resist.

I was a fool earlier thinking I should cave a little to the physical pull between us. I couldn't make up my mind one way or the other, making it impossible to stick to a decision for more than ten minutes. To give him any part of myself before I had my shit figured out would only result in pain.

Wouldn't it?

Shit, I needed to write this stuff on paper. I couldn't even remember the conversations inside my own head. The pros and cons were becoming one giant blur, making me want to yank on my hair and scream out in frustration.

I laid down on my back on the hard floor, my hands clasped together on my stomach, while I stared at the ceiling and tried to regain my sanity. I was literally driving myself insane. I could probably try to talk to someone, get some advice, but that would lead to too many questions. Even Stacy didn't know the full extent of my hang-ups, so to talk to her or anyone else about this would result in me having to hash out shit that was better left buried. Dead and buried.

Despite the chaos ensuing in my mind, it was clear my body had already made up it's mind. My libido wasn't wavering, and made it's point clear at every opportunity. My body wanted him. Bad. I wasn't even sure at this point if resisting him wasn't just making matters worse. All the reasons I distanced myself from men in the past seemed futile and shallow in those moments when he held me. Was lumping Joe in with the rest of them really fair? What would it hurt to give him a chance?

Everything. It would hurt everything.

I picked myself up off the floor, dried my face and turned everything off. Dancing wasn't working, and my studio was a sacred place, so if I couldn't get my mind off of Joe, then I would do my obsessing elsewhere.

Turning to lock the door behind me, I startled when I felt a hand grip my elbow from behind.

"What the hell, Joe?! Why are you here?" I smacked his arm playfully, but he didn't crack a smile. In fact, the seriousness looking back at me made me gulp in apprehension. He studied my face and his mouth tightened when he took in my tear-streaked and puffy face. I was an ugly crier, and the redness in my eyes after crying stayed for hours. Made it harder to hide my emotions, which was why I didn't indulge in a good cry very often.

"I never left. I was just waiting for you to get done so we could talk."

Oh. So he obviously knew I lied about having a class. It didn't seem like he was angry, but I didn't have a clue as to what else would be causing him to act so different than normal. Not wanting to put him in worse of a mood, I didn't pull away when he put his arm around my shoulders and guided me to his truck.

"Wh-where are we going?" *Stuttering. Awesome.*

He didn't answer me, instead just closing the passenger door before going around to his side of his truck. I was starting to feel a little nervous, but I didn't think demanding an answer was going to do any good, so I just stared out the window while we rode in uncomfortable silence. Passivity wasn't something I was all too familiar with, and I'd have loved to reward my newfound maturity with a gold star, but it wasn't truly deserved. I wasn't biting my tongue out of respect, or for any intentional reasons. I was just too messed up at the moment to be confrontational.

I stayed mute the entire drive, taking in my surroundings and staring out the window, painfully aware of every sound made in the quiet cab. The radio was off and other than the hum of the truck's engine, the only other sounds were our breathing. Every now and then I would hear Joe's hands grip the steering wheel, but I was too chicken shit to look at him. I kept my eyes trained on the scene outside the window, looking on with rapt attention as if the view was riveting.

Twenty god-awful, long-ass minutes later we pulled into a suburban neighborhood, of which I assumed was where he lived. I hadn't been to his house, but Stacy had told me about it. The way she described it, I expected to be walking into a modern rendition of Caligula. Apparently Joe had an open door policy with his house and he almost always had visitors. I valued my private time, so

I couldn't possibly fathom why someone would want to live that way.

Just one more major difference between us to add to the list. I was half tempted to pull out my iPhone and type up a pro/con note so I could keep track of these little observances.

Once we were inside his house it was clear that either Stacy grossly over exaggerated, or my imagination was being dramatic. Both scenarios were highly plausible. His front door had a straight view of his sliding glass backdoor, and there were a few people in his pool who looked to be having a good time. The girls were topless, but other than that the scene was pretty tame. A guy was passed out on his couch, and based on the stench of whiskey seeping out of the guys' pores, it didn't take a genius to figure out he was in an alcohol-induced slumber.

I expected beer cans and pizza boxes to be strewn about. My small-minded, judgmental self had apparently been picturing Joe to be living in some sort of adult version of a frat house. I thought I'd see orgies and keg stands and people puking in bushes.

I was actually a little disappointed.

"Alright, everybody out!"

Joe's booming voice startled me, but he immediately put his hand on the small of my back and for reasons unknown to me, I instantly settled. Despite my overactive nerves and wariness from the situation, something in his touch made me feel...safe. Which ironically terrified me.

I stood idly by, enduring the dirty looks of each guest being kicked out of Joe's house. Two more half naked people emerged from the back of his house, and I wondered how well he knew each of these people. Well enough to call each of them by name, it seemed as he gave them all curt goodbyes. One in particular he seemed to know *really* well, because she ran her hand seductively down his torso before grabbing his butt and kissing him on the cheek. Joe tensed, but otherwise didn't react. He didn't return her affections, but he didn't discourage them either.

Ugly jealous flared, and I had never been very good at hiding my emotions, so the venomous look I gave the skank didn't go undetected. She glared right back at me, but when Joe sighed impatiently she made a hasty exit.

Good, I thought. *Back off.*

Shit, I had to knock that crap off.

"Drink?"

Hearing his voice directed at me for the first time since back at my studio made me clam up. My freaking emotions were so all over the place, and I knew if I spoke right then that he would hear a quiver in my voice. Unwilling to make myself feel even more vulnerable, I opted for just shaking my head. He gestured wordlessly for me to sit, and I complied quickly. I didn't like feeling so out of my element, and under normal circumstances that would cause me to react in regrettable ways. Only this time, I found myself wanting to see through the uncomfortableness to find out where it was headed, instead of saying something shitty and storming out.

"My parents died when I was ten."

Odd segue into a conversation, but I figured he had a point for throwing out such a personal, albeit random, detail about himself so I kept my mouth clamped shut.

Damn, I was getting good at holding back. No time for a mental pat on the back. Joe deserved my undivided attention.

"A break-in. Some random drug addict, who fortunately was caught down the road, just looking for something to steal. When he confessed he told the cops that he thought no one was home, and when my dad went after him, he panicked. My parents must have heard something downstairs, because my dad had grabbed his handgun and went to check and that's when it happened.

"I heard the shots, it woke me up. Though I couldn't tell you how many from memory, according to the police report a total of nine rounds had gone off. Only three from my dad's gun, but they all went wide. Apparently there was a struggle, and when my mom heard the shots she must have gone running. It was...it was my dad's gun that shot her. The perp had shot my dad in the stomach during the struggle, the bullet that hit my mom killed her instantly. My dad bled out, probably took hours for him to finally let go."

I fought back a sob, but a few silent tears slipped free without permission. I quickly swiped them away, not wanting Joe to see my reaction, afraid he wouldn't finish if he thought he was upsetting me. He didn't notice. He was staring off into the distance, pain etched in every line of his face.

He cleared his throat and shook his head, bringing him back to the present. "I, um, I was hiding in my closet. Too terrified to come out. I had no idea how long I'd been in there, but I was later told it had been four days. The shooting happened on a Friday night, and it wasn't until Monday evening that someone came to check on us. When I didn't show up to school, and my parents didn't show for work, a patrolman came to check.

"The front door was unlocked, so he let himself in. When he found me I was...I was covered in my own urine and feces, still in the closet. Severely dehydrated and too weak to be embarrassed. They tried to get me out of the house without seeing my parents, but they couldn't move the bodies since it was a crime scene, so they covered them with tarps. I can still picture it in my head though. I could see the outlines of their bodies under the thin plastic, and blood was pooled all around them."

He took a shuttering breath, and I gave in to the urge

and reached out for him. He didn't look at me, but he accepted my hand on his forearm, placing his other hand on top of mine.

"I don't have any other family now, but my maternal grandmother was still alive at the time. I was never really close to her, and living with her didn't change that. I'd had to move here, switching schools, and I didn't know anyone. She took well enough care of me, making sure I had food and clothing, but I was lonely. Until one day the cop who found me came to check on me, and he must have seen something in me that gave away my situation, even though I had tried to put on a brave face.

"He drove me to the community center and introduced me to the staff. Even spent his entire day off there with me, making sure I made some friends and felt comfortable. I started spending all of my free time at the community center, and it was there that I made real friendships. Officer Lyons, that was his name, visited several times over the years. I found out later that he actually kept pretty close tabs on me through a worker at the center. He's the reason I joined the force."

He was quiet for a long time, and I couldn't tell if he was done, but I couldn't hold back the question that had been nagging at me since he started his story.

"Wh-why are you telling me this? Not that I don't want to know, I just mean...it's not like I've been a good friend to you or anything. Hell, I've been more of a bitch than anything. So I just…" I trailed off, not knowing how to explain my confusion.

He finally faced me, and the sincerity and sadness looking at me had me aching to embrace him.

"I'm trying to change that. The friend thing, I mean. I realized I've been handling this all wrong. You're different, Carrie, in the best of ways. But I've been trying to build our friendship the way I would everyone else instead of figuring out a way that would mean something to *you.*"

Well, shit. He just had to go and say the sweetest fucking thing I'd ever heard. "Dammit, Joe," I whined dramatically, making sure he could hear the teasing undertone. I picked up a pen that was sitting on his coffee table and pulled off the cap, leaving it between my teeth while I wrote on his hand. "There, it's official." I snapped the lid back onto the pen while he examined his hand.

"BFFFS?" Joe read the letters aloud questioningly.

"Yep. Best Friends For Fucks Sake."

Joe and I talked for hours after his story about his parents. About his childhood, the parts of mine I was willing to share, and anything and everything else. I didn't know how much longer I was going to be able to keep pretending that my attraction to Joe was something

I could handle. It was easier to resist him when I just thought of him as a sleazy manwhore, but finding out that he's the one the kids always talk about?

That got me deep. I could lie to myself and pretend that the place he was burrowing for himself into my heart was just a friendly affection growing for him, but that would be just that...*a lie*. Physical attraction was manageable, but to develop actual, real feelings for him? *Frack.*

On top of that, my need to get naked with him was becoming so intense that I kept drifting out of the conversation. Every time I would reel my thoughts back in, he would do something mundane - like blink - and I was back to picturing him naked. He turned the channel on the TV - naked. Took a drink of his water - naked. Chewed on his fingernail - naked. You get the point.

I was like a woman possessed. He would shift in his seat and my mouth would water. He'd run his hands through his hair and my heart rate would pick up. I felt like a damn cat in heat, and I finally understood the need people had for relief. My body begged to be brought to orgasm, and I was so wound up that I probably could have rubbed my thighs together a few times and exploded right there in his living room.

I tried to focus on his bad qualities - of which there were few - but no flaw was enough to keep me from hoping he would strip me down and take me right there on his couch, despite the disgusting things that had probably already taken place on it. It was so unlike me to think that way, and part of me felt I should have felt ashamed of myself. I didn't, though, because it's what I seriously wanted. And I knew for a fact, that if he made a move on me again, I wouldn't be able to say no again.

I was so distracted by my thoughts that when he asked if I would like a slice of the pizza he'd ordered, I said yes without thinking. Once I'd taken a bite, I couldn't hold in my moan. It had been *years* since I'd had pizza or anything like it, and it was a horrible idea to be indulging for a number of reasons, but once I'd had a taste I couldn't help but finish the slice.

It wasn't but ten minutes later when I felt the rumblings in my stomach. Joe's concerned eyes darted to mine and I knew he'd heard the growling sounds coming from my angry intestines.

"Bathroom," I blurted out as I bent over, clutching my stomach. Joe had a mouthful of pizza, but he saw my distress and pointed. I took off running, slamming the door closed behind me.

Then quite possibly the most mortifying thing that had happened to me in my entire life...happened. I spent an ungodly amount of time on Joe's toilet, having very noisy and very explosive diarrhea. There wasn't a word in existence to explain my level of humiliation.

I shouldn't have eaten the damn pizza. My body

hadn't had anything greasy in it for so long that my body didn't know how to digest it. *Screw you, bowels!* I'd never hated my traitorous body more than I did in that moment, squatting down on Joe's toilet, afraid to move. Every time I thought my bowels had finally emptied and it was safe to try and get up, my digestive system would flip me off and go on the fritz again.

Point made, bowels! Never again would I indulge in anything that tastes good. It would be twigs and berries for me for the rest of my damn life, because it would be a cold day in hell before I'd relive this experience. Never in my life had I ever regretted anything more, and the cramping had little to do with it.

My stomach was still churning, but it finally decided to show me some mercy and stopped emptying itself. I wasn't in any hurry to face Joe again, but my ass was starting to go numb. I contemplated crawling out his bathroom window, but I'd have to face him eventually, so may as well just get it over with. *After* washing my hands. Thoroughly. *Ugh.*

I eased the door open an inch at a time, hoping upon hope that Joe would be distracted so I would have a little time before facing him. My lesson in humility wasn't done for the day - or I'd earned myself some seriously bad Karma at some point - because when I opened the door wide enough to poke my head out he was standing right outside the bathroom. I was tempted to duck back inside and hide, but the smidgen of pride left in me forced my chin up. *Fake it 'til you make it.*

"Just how long have you been standing there?" As soon as I asked him I decided I didn't want the answer. Thankfully, he gave me a noncommittal answer and held out his hands. My embarrassment took a momentary backseat to my appreciation of Joe's sweet nature when I saw he was holding medicine and a glass of water out for me.

I took them, giving him a hesitant close-mouthed smile, before pounding the final nail in my coffin by blurting out "I washed my hands!"

Joe laughed at my spontaneous and entirely unnecessary admission, before motioning for me to follow him back to the living room. Once again the temptation to run and hide, bury my head in the sand or shout expletives loudly was strong, but before I could do anything at all, Joe started chatting. Like nothing had happened.

A masochistic part of me kept wanting to bring it up and apologize. Wanted him to tease me or make me feel disgusting for what just happened, but I managed to keep myself in check. When he asked me to tell him what the pending deal with Grind was, I jumped on the opportunity to contribute to the conversation without being awkward.

"Well, Reed - the owner, who you know - approached me about an idea she had. She's wanting to expand, build more clubs around the globe and before she does that she wants to make sure she has an edge over the competition. It was a fantastic idea, so I jumped on the opportunity to work with her on it. It's been incredibly stressful, but mostly because it's the first performance, and there will be investors there. I want to make sure we blow her out of the water with what I've put together so that maybe my dancers will get some more regular work."

"So what is it exactly you'll be doing at Grind?"

We'd kept the whole idea a secret and very few people knew what was going to happen. Reed had some fierce competition in her industry, which included a shitton of drama that I didn't know the half of, and she didn't want to risk someone getting the jump on her. Seeing as how the performance was only a couple days away, and Joe seemed pretty trust-worthy, I figured it wouldn't hurt to share it with someone.

"Basically she wants to have dancers employed by the club who perform and then dance with the crowd throughout the night. It's a way to keep people engaged and keep the dance floor busy. It's not really necessary for Grind, but the new clubs she's thinking of opening will be membership only, and the professional dancers in scantily clad outfits will be a perk. They won't be like, hooking up with people or anything. Nothing shady like that. But the membership cost will be hefty and the club will end up with high profile, very rich people who will want to be entertained. Instead of having girls in cages or dancers on stage, she wants dancers who actually engage with the members. It's brilliant, really."

Joe listened intently while I went on to describe more of her plan, adding in his opinion and thoughts once in awhile, showing that he was really listening. It was refreshing, talking to a man who was actually interested in conversing with you and not just getting you naked. Since I didn't date often, instead limiting my intimate experiences with men to mainly the bedroom, it was a nice change of pace.

A few hours and several short trips to the bathroom later, he drove me home. He pulled into a parking spot outside my complex, and I turned to face him, ready to get the apology out of the way. I didn't get a chance though, because Joe immediately took my hand in his and an almost undetectable blush covered his cheeks.

"Thank you for spending time with me today, Carrie. I really do enjoy being around you. I hope we can do this again soon."

I muttered some kind of inaudible agreement, and darted out of his truck like the fucking coward I was.

CHAPTER 9
CARRIE

If anyone cornered me and asked if I'd been obsessing over Joe for the last few days, I would have been forced to say no. At which point, my pants would spontaneously burst into flames. Third degree burns would be a small price to pay to keep my dignity intact. Well, what was left of it after my traitorous bowels went on the fritz.

Luckily, I finally had something else to obsess over. Like how it was the night of the big performance. The one my dancers had been working their asses off for months for to the point of exhaustion. They'd all made it back in time, and everything was set up and ready to go. I wanted so badly to stress over something to pass the time, but it was all done, I had nothing left to prepare.

So I decided to grab a coffee. Not the most exciting of activities, but I couldn't just sit around my apartment and I didn't want to do anything to wear myself out by running or going to the studio. Going on a coffee date with my e-reader for the afternoon seemed like the perfect way to pass the time. And it was working until Lacy walked in the door.

I hadn't seen her since I'd made an ass of myself that day at Grind, but she didn't seem to have any hard feelings towards me. She gave me a friendly smile, which I returned, but the girl with her glared at me murderously when Lacy turned and whispered something into her ear. Then in a flash, Lacy's friend came storming over in my direction. I took a quick glance over her shoulder, and Lacy gave me an apologetic smile.

The ridiculously angry woman made herself comfortable in the chair across from mine. Without invitation, mind you. Her face was all scrunched up like she smelled something bad, and I accidentally laughed. Okay, fine, I didn't even try to hold it back. I couldn't help it. She was trying to act like a snot, but she was just making a fool of herself.

"I just wanted to introduce myself," she said sweetly, a bright smile plastered on her face all of a sudden. *Is this girl bi-polar or something?*

I started to open my mouth, but she cut me off before I got any words out.

"I know who you are." Outwardly she appeared to be cool and collected, but there was a venom in her words that was so strong it was almost palpable. "You're Joe's latest conquest." *Well damn, wasn't expecting that.*

"First off-" I started but was quickly cut off again. I was quickly growing agitated with our one-sided conversation.

"Spare me, honey. I don't know why he's decided to play house with you, but I felt obligated to let you know it won't last. You know, girl code and all." Her carefully placed smile was slipping into a sneer, letting me know this little warning of hers was anything but friendly. "There's only one girl he's ever had repeats with, and that's me. I've been letting him sow his oats so that when he's ready to settle down, I'll know he's all mine. So I'll let him get you out of his system, too, because that's what good girlfriends do."

I sat back and crossed my arms, more than amused with her sad little speech. Did she even hear herself? Good girlfriends let their men sleep with other women? How sad must her childhood have been? She really was quite beautiful, but obviously had very low self-esteem. I would feel sorry for her if she wasn't trying to verbally bitch slap me at the moment.

"Is there a point to all of this?" I waved my hand nonchalantly and rolled my eyes, making sure she understood that she was wasting her time. I could care less what Joe did with his personal life. Okay, that was a lie, but she didn't need to know that.

"Yes, *bitch*, there is a point," she gritted out and hissed a little. Her fake niceties had disappeared and all that remained was the catty, insecure little girl she had been trying so hard to hide. "The point is, don't get comfortable. He *will* leave you, and I will be right there waiting when he does. Because he always comes back to me, and this time is no different."

I watched her leap smugly to her feet and flip her

hair over her shoulder as she walked to the door where Lacy was waiting on her.

"Hey, nice talk! We should do it again sometime!" I yelled, realizing I didn't even get her name. It didn't matter, seeing as how I planned on never talking to her again. Still, I didn't want to make a bad impression or anything, so I gave her a sarcastically innocent smile, snickering to myself when she rolled her eyes.

I wanted to be annoyed that she'd confronted me like that, especially since there was no cause, but really I felt thankful. It was a good reminder of one of the main reasons I didn't do relationships. Everyone has a past, and I was already fighting my own demons. I was in no frame of mind to take on someone else's.

I glanced down at my phone and groaned when I realized it was still only eleven in the morning. I didn't even have to be at Grind until eight that night. I was going to go stir crazy just sitting around all day, and I thought about calling up Stacy or Adalyn, but they both had their own stuff going on. Plus, they would be at the show that night, so I didn't want to bug them even more.

I put my head in my hands and started to massage my temples when the bell over the door to the coffee shop dinged, and I jumped when I felt a tap on my shoulder. Joe laughed as he took the seat his little sex toy had just vacated, and my mouth instantly started watering. Hot damn, he was sexy in his uniform. Really, it was hard to hold it against him how much he slept around.

He was such a contradiction. His face was sexy enough to be on a billboard, and the day old scruff he was sporting gave his otherwise pretty boy features a gruff look. His body was covered in layers of uniform and equipment, but it didn't make it any less obvious that he had a finely sculpted body that he obviously worked hard for. His dark eyes were soul piercing and intense, but his boyish smile made him come across as approach- able and laid back.

So really - how the hell was any woman supposed to resist all of that? And when he clasped his big hands together on the table, I couldn't help but picture them wrapped around a gun. It wasn't that the idea of someone getting shot was a turn on, but it was undeniably sexy when a man was willing to put his own life on the line for others like he did day in and day out.

I imagined those strong hands on me, and I could almost feel one of them tangled in my hair, pulling hard enough to cause the right amount of pain to shoot from my scalp down to my core. I absentmindedly rubbed my wrists as I pictured the other hand pinning my hands above my head while he took my body hard and fast.

I knew I was staring, and I should have felt ashamed of how quickly my chest was rising and falling, my heart speeding up more and more with each second I pictured him taking pleasure from me. I could feel his eyes on me, and I was sure if I looked up at him, he would be smirking at me, but like hell did I care.

It wasn't until my clit started throbbing so badly that I thought I might actually orgasm in a crowded coffee shop, simply from a fantasy, that I forced my attention back into the present.

"Need a moment of privacy?" Joe teased. I was sure he expected me to blush or be embarrassed that I'd been openly ogling him, but I wasn't. If he wasn't offended that I had been visually molesting him, then he could get over it, because he'd been doing it to me for months.

Mustering up confidence from somewhere way, way deep inside of me, I managed a response that actually came across as nonchalant. "No, I'll finish that fantasy at home when I'm in bed and can enjoy it properly." Joe choked harshly when he sucked in a sharp breath, clearly surprised by my blunt honesty. Since I'd unconsciously decided to forget all the reasons sex with Joe was a bad idea, I had no qualms being a giant tease. I was no prude, and up until that very moment Joe had never seen this side of me.

"And what fantasy is that?" He asked after taking a sip of the water that a concerned waitress had brought over to him while he had his coughing fit. She had tried to shove her ample chest in his face as she did it, but he waved her off, not even noticing.

"Oh, I was just picturing you holding my wrists

above my head while you fucked me up against a wall." I shrugged and took a drink of my coffee to hide the laugh I was fighting when his jaw hit the table.

"Ehhem, well, that's not what I...I didn't think...I mean, you…" A man being unsure and stuttering over himself would have been unattractive on anyone else, but seeing someone as sure of himself as Joe get tongue-tied over me was heady. The feeling of power it gave me, knowing I could get under his skin, made it easier to slink into denial. I pushed those pesky voices in my head that were trying to reason with me to stop the game I was starting so far into the background that my only goal became seeing just how far I could push him.

"Sorry, you asked. If you didn't want to know that I was imagining what your hands would feel like as they caressed my nipples, then you shouldn't have asked." I reached out and took one of his hands in both of mine, turning it palm up, and rubbing it lightly with the tip of my index finger. "Hmmm, that's what I thought," I muttered to myself.

"Wh-what did you think?"

"I just wondered if your trigger finger would be a little rough right here," I said as I rubbed a small circle on the inside of his index finger. "Up close, it's easier to imagine how capable your hands probably are beyond taking down dangerous criminals. I would be much easier to overpower, but I'd put up a good fight. Although, that might make it a little more rewarding for you once you get me pinned to the bed, straddle my waist and cuff me to the headboard. Tell me, Joe. Once I'm at your mercy, what will you do with me?"

Joe swallowed hard, and I smiled as I pulled the handcuffs I had discreetly slipped off his belt over the table, snapping one closed around his wrist. His eyes went wide, and for a second I could have sworn I saw anger floating around, but it was gone in a flash. I toyed with the empty cuff, biting my lip seductively. It wasn't subtle, but then, I wasn't trying to be.

"When do you get off?" I could have asked when his shift was over, but the loud gulp and stuttering response was exactly the kind of reaction I was looking for.

"Not until eight," he replied, his eyes locked on my hand while I continued fingering the cuffs.

"Aww, too bad. I had time to kill. Thought we could turn one of those fantasies into reality. Oh well. Another time." I shrugged casually, and when I stood up he finally regained his composure and realized I'd been screwing with him.

"Well played, half pint." He winked, showing me he's not angry at my teasing.

"Advantage, Carrie," I said as I walked backwards, and I was thankful to be facing him when he looked up. An evil grin formed slowly and his eyes darkened, challenging me without words. I almost tripped over myself, because never in my life had a man made me go weak in the knees with just a look. Until now.

"Not for long." He might have said the words out loud, but I couldn't hear past the blood rushing in my head. I read his lips well enough, though, and knew I had just thrown down some kind of gauntlet. Repercussions be damned. I was done holding back.

"Bring it!"

"Where is Jillian!"

I was freaking out. I wanted to be in control of myself and prove that I could handle myself in a crisis, but that wasn't going to happen. Not right then. Not when everything was on the verge of falling apart.

"If someone doesn't get Jillian on the phone or in front of my face in the next five seconds I'm going to lose my shit!"

Everyone heard me screaming at the top of my lungs, but no one responded. They were all frantically trying to find Jillian while I paced back and forth backstage. I was cursing under my breath and chewing on my nails, a nervous habit I never could break, when Stacy came waltzing in.

"Whuddup, snatch face!"

My head flew up and over so fast I almost got whiplash. One look and Stacy knew I was not in the mood.

"Whoa, what the fuck did I just walk into?" Stacy approached me cautiously, like I was a rabid animal. Smart. "Someone please clue me in on why my best friend looks like she could easily commit a mass murder with no remorse."

When no one spoke up, I rolled my eyes. "Jillian isn't here." Shock and understanding morphed Stacy's face, and I turned away before I could see pity. Everything was ruined if Jillian didn't show up and she knew it. Jillian was the main dancer, the star of the performance. I had backup dancers who could step in easily for anyone else. Anyone but Jillian. I'd searched and searched, but could never find someone who could match her skill. She was one of a kind.

"You do it."

Stacy's suggestion didn't shock me; it was something I'd considered. After all, I knew the dance better than anyone, but I was supposed to be with Reed during the performance. Overseeing the crowd and taking in their response, and if her reaction was less than enthusiastic I wanted to be there to help convince her we could make it better.

"I can't. I'm supposed to be sitting with Reed and investors in the new VIP room during the performance. I'm not a dancer in this arrangement. My involvement is strictly from a business owner standpoint."

"There won't *be* a performance to watch if you

don't have someone up there to perform."

Valid point.

"We found her!" Lawrence's voice rang out from behind me. He was more like a partner than a dancer, always helping me with just about every aspect of the studio. My second in command, and at that moment, my personal savior. I ran over to him and started peppering his face with kisses, but he put his hands on my shoulders and pushed me back. His face said it all.

"Fuck!" He winced, but to his credit, he didn't back away. He was one of few dancers I worked with who weren't afraid of me. It wasn't something I was proud of. I was exceptionally difficult to work with, another part of me I was trying to work on.

"The subway train she's on broke down. She will make it here, but probably not until after the performance has started. So unless you can stall, then you've gotta go on for her baby girl."

We couldn't delay the performance. Reed and her investors were busy people, and minutes of their time were more valuable than a week of mine. Any delays would look really badly upon not only myself, but Reed, and it could cost us everything we'd worked towards.

"Where are you going!?" Lawrence called after me when I stormed off.

"To the damn fitting room! Get everyone ready. The show must go on!"

JOE

I was trying feign cool indifference at the thought of getting to see Carrie perform, but Stacy saw right through my bullshit. Thankfully she didn't call me out on it, but I know she didn't miss my reaction when she told me one of the dancers wasn't there and that Carrie was going to have to step up in her place.

I hadn't admitted it to Carrie, or anyone else for that matter, but after I'd left her studio, I'd hung around like a creeper and watched her dance through the door. Mesmerized, entranced, whatever girly bullshit word you want to use for someone who can't tear their eyes away from something, that was me.

I'd never seen someone's body move the way hers did. Her tiny frame contorted in ways that shouldn't even be possible, and when she would extend her arms and legs in the most graceful way imaginable, I felt my heart feeling shit it shouldn't. Things it had no business feeling when it came to her. Someone who was most definitely unattainable, no matter how hard it was for me to admit.

Still, knowing I couldn't have her may have been

part of the lure at times, but in that moment it was the furthest thing from my mind. I could have stood there for hours, watching her sway and dip and twirl across the floor effortlessly. I imagined what it would feel like to be standing next to her when she extended her toned leg straight up in the air, where I could graze my fingertips from her ankle down to her inner thigh.

I could almost feel the smoothness of her skin and my fingers tingled at the imagined sensation. The image of that same leg wrapped around my neck while I used my mouth to search her most intimate places had my dick so hard I thought the button on my pants might pop off.

The logical part of me was telling me to walk away and end the torture, but when Carrie dropped to her knees and rolled on the ground, arching her back and pushing her chest towards the ceiling...my life flashed before my eyes. My heart flat lined, all the air swooshed out of my lungs, and it wasn't until she finally stopped dancing that I felt like I could actually breathe.

When my heart started to beat again, something had changed. Like someone who died and came back to life, I felt like I had a renewed sense of self. Carrie had been doing a number on me from the start, but for whatever reason, it was that moment in time that I both consciously and subconsciously admitted that what I was feeling was much deeper than lust.

It was that admission that gave me the courage to tell her about my parents' death, something I had never discussed with anyone. I hadn't let on how painful it had been to talk about, and not because of any misguided need to be manly or some shit. I just knew if I let my emotions show at all, I would have fallen apart, and it would have destroyed the point I was trying to make.

I wanted to open up to her in hopes that she would let me in. It worked...somewhat. She hadn't returned the gesture and divulged me of any uber private details, but she'd stayed. She let her guard down enough to engage in conversation, and if I wasn't mistaken, actually enjoyed herself. It was progress, a step forward.

Maybe it made me pathetic, like a dog begging for scraps, to accept whatever little amounts of herself she decided to give me. But my gut told me she was worth it, and that as painful as the journey might be, if I made it across that finish line with her I knew I wouldn't have any regrets.

Getting to see her perform wasn't something she was voluntarily showing me, but it was still a glimpse into her life. A piece of who she was. If she danced tonight anything like I'd seen in private, then that's exactly what she would be doing. Giving everyone in the crowd a little piece of herself. Maybe I only noticed because I couldn't tear my eyes off of her. The lights, the other dancers, the crowd...they all disappeared when Carrie took the stage. Maybe I noticed it because I was looking for it, looking for something more than the surface level most people saw.

Part of me wanted to believe I really was the only one who would see so deeply into her soul. That it meant we had some sort of deeper connection that provided me that little window into a side of her not everyone got to see. Whether or not that was true, and whether anyone saw what I did or not, she was going to expose herself. I wasn't imagining the changes in her when she moved to the music. When she danced she put it all out there...her heart, soul and pain...it's what made it so beautiful.

Whatever I'd anticipated seeing was blown away when she actually started to perform. From the second the lights dropped and she was slowly lowered from the high ceiling down to the crowd, the whole audience was enraptured. The black shorts she wore looked more like underwear than clothes, and the lace bodice clung to her like a second skin. She sparkled and glistened, and she was fiercely sexy. I knew every other man in the place was visually devouring her just like I was, and while at least a dozen other dancers soon joined in, I couldn't tear my gaze from her.

I was close enough to the stage to know she was entirely focused and in character for the dance, but it didn't stop me from feeling as if she were dancing just for me. Every thrust of her hips, every seductive stare and every sultry bend her body made felt as if it were specifically choreographed for my own personal enjoyment.

Dancers left the stage and snaked through the crowd, engaging them in dance and getting everyone pumped up. The energy in the place was off the charts, you could feel it thrumming through the air. The more worked up the crowd got, the more I was bumped and knocked into, but my eyes never left her. Not for a second.

I watched intently as she made her way down the stage, into the crowd, and straight to me. In all my staring, I could have sworn she hadn't even noticed me, but she had to have known where I was standing because she moved like a woman with a mission.

The smile she gave me when she slipped her arms around my neck and started to dance had all my blood rushing to one location. She turned her back to me, bent at the waist and rolled her body against me, making my dick swell to a point of pain. The more she danced, grinding her ass against my erection, the more it continued to grow. It had to have been twice it's normal size by the time she strutted away, joining the rest of the dancers on stage for the finale.

I didn't even try to be subtle when adjusting myself, not giving two shits if anyone noticed, though I doubted anyone would. Everyone, men and women alike, were enthralled by the performance. And when it ended, the club erupted in cheers and applause loud enough to shake the walls. After a quick bow, the dancers retreated behind a black curtain, and my feet were moving before my brain caught on to where I was headed.

Taking things slow was no longer possible. My whole plan to win her over as a friend before pursuing her again was shot to hell after that performance. I needed her. *Now.*

CHAPTER 10
CARRIE

Backstage was chaos. Everyone was celebrating, popping champagne, excitedly recounting the details of everything. Adrenaline was coursing through my veins, giving me a high I only ever felt from being on stage. It had been too damn long since I'd gotten to experience it, and it was like a recovered junkie taking their first hit. I felt completely, and utterly drugged.

I took it all in, reveling in the success. I knew Reed would be pleased, because even from the stage where the lights were too blinding to really take in my surroundings, I knew the crowd was going wild. Their energy was a living, breathing life form, and it only fueled the dancers. Myself included.

After a few minutes spent congratulating all my dancers, I saw a dark form hidden in the shadows out of the corner of my eye. I couldn't see who it was, but somehow I knew. It was like his body called out to mine, and before I knew what was happening, I was running to him. Like, full out running with no hint of stopping.

I closed the short distance in seconds, and when I was close enough I took a blind leap of faith and threw myself at him. His strong arms caught me easily and I wrapped my body around his, threaded my fingers through his hair and pulled his mouth to mine.

I needed to release some of the energy still building up inside of me, and if I was truly honest with myself, my first thought after running backstage was Joe. I wanted to run to him and celebrate, share my moment with him and only him. It was a thought that should have sent me running, and it did. Only this time it sent me running right to him, and thank God, he was ready for me.

Months of pushing him away, denying my feelings and fighting so hard to remain in control just evaporated. It felt exhilarating and liberating and terrifying, but dancing tonight had given me clarity. Life was a risk, and I couldn't keep running. I thought I was brave, that my independence somehow meant I was being smart, but I'd only been hiding. Like a coward.

I knew Joe could feel it, my surrender, as we kissed. What had started as hurried and hungry turned into a slow caress as Joe worshiped my mouth with his. I let myself go, hoping he could feel the shift in me through my kiss, and when he pulled away I whimpered, my lips chasing his. His hand gripped my chin, forcing my eyes to open and look at him, and I didn't like the seriousness staring back at me.

Worry and apprehension started to creep in, but the ache between my legs didn't lessen, even as he put me back on my feet and took a step away from me. If anything, it got worse. Joe standing so close to me, within reaching distance, but not feeling like I could reach out and touch him was torture.

I wanted to throw myself at him again just to keep him from opening his mouth. If what he was about to say was that I shouldn't have jumped on him, and that us kissing was a mistake, then I didn't want to hear it.

"No more games, Carrie. No more running away. I've let you tease me with that wicked mouth for the last time. This is your last warning, your last chance to walk away, because if you stay...your body is mine. And not just your body, and most certainly not for one night. So think before you kiss me again, because my control, my patience, is withering."

He wasn't exaggerating, I could see him fight to restrain himself. His fists clenching so hard his knuckles went white, his chest heaving up and down while his teeth ground against each other so harshly I could hear it.

His warning...no, his threat...would normally have ended with me kicking him in his nuts. To let a man own me, take what he wants from me whenever and however he pleased, was a thought that always sickened me. Yet hearing it come from Joe, I found myself unbelievably turned on. I wanted to be his, to belong to him.

Because I trusted him. Seeing a flying, rainbow-colored unicorn would have been more believable than me trusting a man, but I did. I knew he wouldn't just take his own pleasure. No, a man like Joe would give before he took anything in return. He would relish in the feeling of knowing that my pleasure belonged to him, because he would be the one taking me there. And he would take me there, over and over, until I couldn't take any more.

My want for him morphed into a desperate need, and my body swayed toward him. Like an invisible tether was pulling me towards a future I'd never even dared to dream of, and I finally let go, and took my first step towards him. Towards the unknown.

I placed my palms flat on his hard chest, one directly over his heart, and looked up into his eyes. Dark, wanting eyes stared back at me, and the air thinned. I felt dizzy with desire, licking my dry lips, an invitation for him to take what was now his.

"There you are!"

I didn't turn to look at Reed, too entranced with Joe to look away, until she reached out and touched my arm. I knew she was there, but it still startled me, and the knowing look she gave me said she knew exactly what she interrupted.

"So sorry, but can I steal you away for a few minutes? One of the potential investors would like to speak with you, as well as some other figureheads who, after seeing how wonderful of a show you put on, are looking to possibly get in on this as well."

"Of course." I started to follow Reed, knowing full well that being alone with Joe right then was a bad idea.

Not because it was a mistake, but because I was two seconds away from clawing at his body and begging him to take me right there. I didn't want to leave things totally unfinished, though, so with Joe's threat repeating itself in my head, I walked back over to him. I placed a soft, chaste kiss on his lips, pulling away too quickly for him to be able to return it.

I took slow steps backwards towards Reed, wanting to make sure Joe understood what I'd meant with that kiss. And if the scorching way his eyes looked me over from head to toe, like he was planning all the ways he wanted to claim me, was any indication, then he definitely got the message loud and clear.

I was so damn exhausted. Turned out Reed wanting me to talk to the investors was a ruse, and when we got to the room, it was actually a surprise party. I was moved, to say the least, because it meant that all along everyone had believed I would be able to pull this off.

The investors were there, among my dancers and several other people I didn't know. Ian stopped by just long enough to congratulate me and let me know Adalyn needed to get home and off her feet. Stacy and Chad stayed about a half hour, but had to leave so he could rest for his early shift.

I spent an absurd amount of time looking for Joe,

but apparently he hadn't come. I checked my phone more times than I care to admit, but no text explaining his absence. I tried so hard to stay in the moment and bask in the glory of it all, but my mind kept wandering to Joe, and despite the celebration I couldn't help but feel disappointed.

I thought for sure Joe knew what I meant with that kiss. I hated questioning myself or having doubts about my actions. I didn't act impulsively very often because I didn't like living with regrets, and the first time in I don't even know how long I put myself out there, then... nothing.

I spent the whole night fighting my insecurities, warring inside of myself, trying to avoid slipping into old patterns. I didn't need Joe to feel good about myself, I didn't need any man for that. So why was I feeling so damn dejected?

After what I felt was a reasonable amount of time, I finally claimed exhaustion and left the party. It wasn't a lie, I really was exhausted. The adrenaline had worn off, and my overactive mind was wearing me down. By the time I made it to my apartment building, my body was begging to be put into a hot bath, then retreat to the comfort of my big, fluffy bed.

It wasn't until I was in the hallway of my place that I realized the door handle hadn't actually been locked when I turned my key. I froze mid-step, trying to figure out if I should grab the big umbrella perched against the wall next to me and face my intruder, or just take off running.

After being frozen in time for several seconds, which actually felt more like minutes, I finally decided to make a run for it. I didn't even make it a step before a firm hand wrapped around my wrist and yanked me back, pushing me up against the wall, then pinning my hands above my head. My eyes squeezed shut, too afraid to face my attacker, I opened my mouth to scream but a hand clamped over it, muffling the sounds.

"Carrie. Carrie! Carrie, look at me." I heard a voice from far away, saying my name over and over when I stopped trying to scream. My body slowly started to relax, and a deep breath in gave way to recognition. My eyes popped open and were greeted by Joe's, which were full of amusement as he tried not to laugh.

"You asshole!" I yelled when his hand fell away from my mouth, and I hit him as hard as I could on his arm. "You scared the shit out of me! How did you even get in here?!" My pounding heart sent blood rushing through my veins like a tidal wave, making me dizzy, but it wasn't from fear. As soon as I realized it was Joe up against my body, fear turned into powerful, all-consuming lust.

"I'm sorry," he said as his laughs died down, and amusement turned to something akin to reverie. He cupped my cheek in the palm of his hand and closed the gap between us, his body pressing mine firmly against the wall. He opened his mouth to say something, but I wasn't in the mood for talking. My oversensitive nerves were screaming for relief, and no amount of talking was going to make it any better.

JOE

I'd scared her, and a better man would have taken a minute to help her calm down. Comfort her. Not shove his tongue down her throat and start tearing off her clothes.

Every damn day I did my best to be a good man, but right that minute, good or bad was irrelevant. I just wanted to be *her* man.

I need to feel her. All of her. Never in my life had I so desperately wanted someone. I felt trapped in my own skin, captive to my own urges. My blood boiled, my skin burning from the inside out, and I knew with absolute certainty that if I didn't feel her naked body underneath of mine within the next few minutes, there was a very good chance I would actually combust.

Thanking God for whatever good karma I had earned in the past, I groaned with gratitude when she reacted just as frantically. The times I'd felt her soft lips on mine in the past were memories I called upon frequently, but even those paled in comparison to the way she was ravishing my mouth as vigorously as I was hers.

Somewhere deep inside I knew I should slow down, be gentler with her, but I couldn't stop. She didn't seem to mind when I grabbed a fistful of her hair and yanked her head back so I could devour her neck, if her moan of pleasure was any indication.

"Bedroom," she muttered-slash-moaned as she pushed my chest with the palms of her hands. I never pulled my mouth from her skin, walking backwards with her guidance, and multi-tasking like a freaking pro as I also continued stripping both of us.

By the time the back of my knees hit her bed, we were both stark naked. I fell backwards, my mouth already missing the feel of her, my hands twitching as I resisted the urge to reach out and touch her.

Leaning back on my hands, I drank her in, knowing I would never forget the glorious perfection that stood before me. Even when I turned old and gray, and even if all other memories had escaped me, I knew I would still remember what Carrie looked like in that moment. My skin tingled while I let her take her time getting her own fill of my body, relishing in the knowledge that just looking at me was sending chills throughout her body.

She shivered, and though I knew it wasn't from the cold, I used it as my excuse to reach out and grab her.

She squealed joyfully when I yanked her down on top of me, laughing as I rolled us over so that I was hovering above her.

I forced myself to slow down for a fraction in time, just long enough to assess her face and body language, to confirm that it was what she wanted. When she growled impatiently, I finally let go. There was nothing sweet or gentle, and though I knew I should worship her like she deserved, I couldn't help myself. A primal need had taken over me, and it felt as though I was no longer in control of my own body.

Like the selfish asshole I was, I thrust into her without even checking to see if she was ready for me. Much to my delight, I slid in easily, and each time I would pull out to the tip and thrust back inside was more amazing than the last. I had to bite down on the inside of my cheek to keep from exploding the minute I entered her, which would have been the most mortifying thing I could have done.

Thankfully, I was able to keep myself together, and I was even more thankful when I felt her walls already contracting around my shaft tightly. Her back arched and her nails dug into my shoulders, and I knew she was close already.

Everything was perfect. Exactly as I'd imagined it. Until she started chanting "Oh God, oh God," over and over again.

"What are you doing?" I stopped moving and hovered over her on my forearms. It took her a second to realize I was still, and staring at her expectantly. When she finally opened her eyes, her whole face turned a deep shade of red, all the way from the tips of her ears to the tips of her breasts.

"Wh-what do y-you mean?"

I climbed off of her and started getting dressed. Out of the corner of my eye I saw her pulling the sheet up to her neck, clutching it by her chest.

"Where are you going? What is happening right now?" I hated the uncertainty in her voice, but I wasn't going to take the blame for acting like an ass right now. This had never happened to me before, and I wasn't even sure how to broach the subject.

She looked down at my softening erection, and gave me a look of understanding that made my last thread of self-control snap.

"Yeah, hard to have sex without an erection, huh?" I deadpanned. "Also hard to have an erection when the woman you're fucking is faking an orgasm."

That deep red blush returned, and for a second I thought she was considering hiding under the blankets. I had wanted to handle this delicately, knowing that Carrie could run for the hills at the slightest complication, but my ego wasn't as patient as the rest of me.

"I-I'm...I don't...I wasn't..."

"Don't lie to me!" I hadn't meant to yell, and her flinch made me feel like an ass, but I was too worked up to change course now. "I can't possibly understand why you would fake an orgasm, especially when you were right on the brink of having a real one, so why don't you explain it to me. You were right there, Carrie, just seconds away from me taking you over the edge. I could feel it, I could see it. So what's with the theatrics?"

Embarrassment turned to anger, and I saw her shutting down. She threw the sheet off and started to get dressed, and I discreetly edged my way to the door so I could block her if she tried to bolt, because there was no way in hell I was going to let this go unfinished.

"You should go, this was a mistake," she bit out.

"More lies. Why don't you do both of us a favor and stop trying to bullshit yourself out of this relationship."

"Relationship!? You think just because I let you put your dick in me one time, not even to completion, that that means we're somehow involved?"

She was panicking, though she was hiding it well behind her anger. But even if I hadn't undergone extensive training that gave me the ability to read people really well, I would *still* know she was panicking, because dammit, I knew *her*.

"No, I don't think that just because I, as you so eloquently put it, 'put my dick in you.' Don't want to call it a relationship? Fine. Call it whatever you want. But don't try to get me to buy into your bullshit of trying to pretend that what this is between us is more than sex. You want to keep lying to yourself, fine, but I'm done letting you try and lie to *me*. And that orgasm you just tried to fake, is a lie."

She was fully dressed and marching my way, and she looked so damn cute, all determined and confident, as if she had a chance in hell of getting past me. "Move, asshat," she ordered.

"Tell me why you were faking it and I will."

"No." She crossed her arms, and I did the same. She wasn't giving in? Well neither was I. We could stand there all damn night for all I cared.

"You are the most infuriatingly stubborn woman I have ever encountered, but if you think I'm going to let you leave here before you explain then you are crazier than Stacy."

"Let me leave? This is my fucking apartment! And what makes you think I was faking it? Are you like, the 'Orgasm Whisperer' or something?" She hadn't meant it as a compliment, but I smirked anyway.

"'Orgasm Whisperer'...I like it!"

"Oh for Christ's sake," she muttered, throwing her arms up in the air. "Yes, okay! Yes, I was faking it. Only because I wanted to hurry the damn process along."

"Bullshit."

"Oh my gosh! Please, Joe, just let me leave." The

fight was leaving her, and if I thought she would eventually tell me the truth, I'd let her have her space. But I knew if I let her walk out that door then I would lose my chance, so I crossed my arms and widened my stance. When she realized she was stuck with no escape, I watched her body deflate as defeat sunk in.

"Ah! Fine! I can't have an orgasm, okay!? You happy? There's the truth. The humiliating and sad truth of my life."

I didn't need to be in front of a mirror to know I looked like a damn fool, standing there staring at her with my mouth gaping open, but *shit*...that was not at *all* what I was expecting.

"You've never had an orgasm? *Ever?*"

Her hands were covering her face, but she dropped them to glare at me. "Of course I've had one, but they've always been self-induced. I've just never had one with a man. I have some sort of mental blockage. I get close, and I chase it, but once I get to the peak of the mountain I can never manage to make it over to the other side."

I ran my hands through my hair, trying to figure out how to process this nugget of information. I was thinking like a selfish asshole, and yeah I was in shock a little, but really all I could think about was that I was going to be the first one to give her an orgasm. And that information had me doing a happy little jig inside, so I ran my hands through my hair again, buying myself some time to compose myself before I did something stupid, like fist pump the air.

When I felt it was safe to respond, I turned to face her. "But why fake it? Just because other guys didn't know how to work their dicks doesn't mean I don't. Trust me, half pint. I could get you there."

She rolled her eyes at me and let out a sarcastic laugh. "I gave up on that a long time ago. Men don't think about anything but getting their own. They don't have the patience or determination to care about my pleasure, so I give them what they want and then give *myself* what I want."

"There are so many things wrong with that explanation that I don't even know where to begin." I thought for a second about how to broach a subject that was obviously difficult for her to discuss, but there was no delicate way to say it, so I just went for it. "If you think that men only care about their own pleasure, then you've only been sleeping with assholes. A real man takes pleasure in pleasing the woman, not just his own release. And if you never orgasm, why even bother with sex to begin with?"

"Oh my God, this is so embarrassing," she muttered. I feigned patience while she warred with herself, but it was taking everything in me to keep from tossing her on the bed and showing her how sex is *supposed* to be. "I enjoy sex. I want sex. I get turned on like anyone else. I guess I kind of hope one of these times it will be different, but so far it hasn't been. And after my asshole of an ex…"

She trailed off and I wanted for her to continue, but when it was obvious she wasn't going to, I cleared my throat to get her attention. I nodded and narrowed my eyes, and she deflated even more, sitting down on the edge of the bed. I waited a second, unsure of whether or not I should stay in place, but ended up deciding to join her and sat down next to her.

"Stan was my high school boyfriend, we'd started dating my freshman year. Like any teenage boy, he'd been wanting to have sex for years, but I hadn't been ready. He was okay with it and never pressured me, but I made the decision junior year that I was ready. He was a year older than me, so he was able to book a hotel and everything, and we planned to do it prom night. Cliché, I know, but it felt right at the time."

"Anyway, a week before prom my mom died. She'd been sick for a while after my dad left us, and we thought it was just depression, but turns out she had syphilis. The doctors said she'd had it for years and it had slowly started to deteriorate her brain, but she was always drunk so we just thought the crazy ramblings were from the alcohol. We didn't know."

She swiped a tear from her cheek, and I had no idea where this was going, but I sat quietly and waited for her to gain her composure. The urge to reach out and take her hand in mine was too strong to fight, and when she immediately twined her fingers through mine, my chest expanded with relief.

"She would go on these rants about how my dad was a cheating asshole. He never contacted us after he left, so we assumed that's what ended their marriage. Then finding out she died from an STD that he gave her...I just didn't have any desire to have sex. It was the last thing on my mind. But he guilted me, saying he already paid for the hotel and he'd been patient and was getting tired of waiting, so…"

"Carrie," I said as I took her other hand in mine, forcing her to look in my eyes. "Did he...did he hurt you?"

She hesitated, and I swear my heart stopped. "What? Oh, God no. Nothing like that." I let out a breath I didn't know I'd been holding and waited for her to keep going.

"He didn't force himself on me, I went willingly, but my heart wasn't in it. Plus, it was my first time so it hurt like hell and an eager teenage boy is anything but gentle. Anyway, after a few minutes of me just laying there he got frustrated. I guess my not being into it was a turnoff, and honestly I just wanted it to be over, so I started faking it. I'd seen movies or shows on late night television where women were having sex, so I mimicked them. It must have worked, because he bought it.

"I dumped him after that. He tried to pressure me

again and I wasn't numb anymore from the shock of my mom dying so I came to my senses and broke it off. My next boyfriend, though...God, this sucks. I've never told anyone this. Not even Stacy. And now I know why. So freaking embarrassing."

"Hey." I took her chin between my fingers and tipped her face up, pressing a light kiss to her lips. "Don't ever be afraid to share with me. Nothing you say will change anything, and I would never betray your trust." She must have believed me, because she seemed to find some courage and kept going.

"Brad, the asshole you met at the bar the first time we met? We were together a long time. He tried, he really did, and he tried *everything*. I mean, we even did some really kinky stuff that I, to this day, am a little shocked I even did, but we got desperate. He would spend...*gah*... he would spend hours going down on me. We got books and even talked to a doctor to see if my parts were like, not functioning correctly or something. They are, by the way. He didn't know it at the time, but I'd been consulting a therapist, who told me Brad was the issue. He was very controlling, never wanting me to show off in public or dress sexy. I didn't really, anyway, but it pissed me off to no end that he felt he had the right to boss me around. After about six months of him trying to please me, while simultaneously bossing me around every chance he got, I finally broke it off with him. He was starting to get resentful and cruel. I think it was taking a toll on his ego that I didn't enjoy sex with him, but my self-esteem wasn't low enough for me to keep putting up with his bullshit. Needless to say, it didn't end well."

She shrugged casually, as if that whole story was just no big deal, but it was. A big freaking deal.

"So you've *never* had an orgasm?"

"Oh, I've had them, but only on my own. I kept seeing that same therapist and she explained that I have a mental block that keeps me from letting go enough to climax. Something about trust and intimacy issues, but that didn't help at all. After enduring two extremely shitty boyfriends, I just couldn't get close enough to someone to get to that level of trust. Fearing they would run the other way once they knew my problem was always in the back of my mind, discouraging me from opening up. But I enjoy sex, enjoy how powerful I feel when a man falls apart in the bed with me. I've just accepted the fact that *I'll* never be the one falling apart. No one has cared, or noticed, until you."

"Okay, just to make sure I'm hearing you correctly...you're saying the only person who can give you an orgasm is yourself?"

"Yes."

"Challenge accepted."

CHAPTER 11
CARRIE

"Joe is a cuddler."

I spat that little tidbit out right before taking a sip of my coffee, which resulted in Stacy choking on her own.

"What the hell? When did this happen?"

"Last night. And can you keep your voice down? I don't really want to share with the whole cafe that I had my first orgasm from sex last night."

After another bout of coughing, Stacy snatched up her purse and yanked me out of my seat. "What the-"

"Nope, not having this conversation here. This is something you discuss over shots of tequila, not mocha lattes."

"Stacy, it's only eleven in the morning." I didn't know why I thought pointing out the time would make a difference, because the time of day sure as hell had never mattered to Stacy.

"It's two o'clock somewhere, and that's when my day drinking usually starts. We're just being over achievers. Plus, I need your help with something on the way to my house."

When we reached the corner of the crosswalk, Stacy pulled a stack of papers and a staple gun out of her over-sized bag.

"Uhhhhhh…" Stacy stapled one of the sheets of paper to a lamppost before I could ask her what the hell she was doing. Then she shoved the staple gun in my hand, and pulled out a second one. "Do you always carry around weaponized hardware?"

I took a closer look at the paper on the post and tried to hold back a frustrated scream, which made it come out sounding like a strangled cry. It earned me a few strange looks from passersby, but weird noises coming out of me on the street was nothing compared to what Stacy was plastering over half the city.

"Hurry up, snatchface! We've got three hundred of these babies to get up and we gotta do it fast!"

"You know, I'd really appreciate more of a heads up before you enlist me in your harebrained schemes." I complained as I caught up to Stacy.

"If I had told you, would you have helped?"

"No."

"Well, there ya go." She was too focused on getting her homemade posters up to even argue with me. I'd never seen her so determined, and if what she was working on was even *somewhat* of a good thing, I would have been impressed. But this is Stacy we're talking about - she only threw herself into things that were absolutely, off the charts stupid.

"We might have to run by Ian's office to make more copies."

"Does he even know you used his company resources for the first three hundred you printed?"

"Of course not. Now stop your yappin', and get to helpin'. Gerard's not gonna find himself."

I rolled my eyes and got to work. I knew she was going to keep hanging the posters, with or without my help, and I really needed to talk about Joe, so helping would only get it done faster. Forty minutes later I hung up my last poster. "What do you hope to accomplish by hanging up hundreds of posters with a picture of your missing dildo on them? That's not even your phone number on there. Whose is that?"

Realization dawned on me when she gave me an evil smirk. Originally when I'd first seen the picture of a dildo I didn't even bother looking at all of it, figuring the less I knew the better. *Wrong*. I should have looked. I wanted absolutely nothing to do with this.

"Stacy, please tell me this is not Chad's phone number underneath where it says 'My beloved dildo and I have shared many wonderful and enjoyable memories, and I miss him very much. If you see him, please call Officer Sexy Pants. Reward will be substantial.'"

Stacy didn't answer, she just snickered and hung up the last poster she was holding. "Alright, I think that's enough. Should do the trick."

"What makes you so sure anyone is even going to call him?" I asked, watching Stacy glance down at her phone. She spared a sarcastic look in my direction that told me she thought my question was stupid.

"Of course people are going to call him. Fifty bucks, he has to change his phone number before dinner. Thanks for helping babe," she said as she slung an arm over my shoulders. "We're only a few minutes away from my house now. Let's go get shit-faced and gossip about men," she said as she wiggled her eyebrows up and down excitedly.

I followed close behind her, and I did not like how bouncy she was as she walked. She was way too proud of herself. Chad hated to lose control of himself, and Stacy just loved to push his buttons. They were such a nightmare together, and yet somehow, they worked.

We were sitting at a table sipping coffee, and I listened as Stacy explained her entire plan to get even with Chad for kidnapping Gerard. "So how did you find an exact picture of your actual dildo?"

"I already had one," she said casually.

"Wait...huh? Why would you have stock photos of your dildo already?"

Stacy sighed impatiently at me. "No, that picture *is* Gerard. It's one I took," she replied with a roll of her eyes.

"Why the hell would you take a picture of your dildo?"

She shrugged and answered simply, "They say you

should take pictures of your valuables in case anything is ever stolen."

Some days I had to seriously ask myself how in the hell Stacy and I were friends. Today was one of those days. Stacy's phone rang, and when she looked down at it she smiled the biggest smile I'd ever seen on her and held her phone up for me to see.

"There's no name. Who is it?" She held up a finger and clicked 'accept.'

"Why hello there, Officer Man Candy, how is your day going so far?" She was practically singing, she was so giddy. Stacy put him on speakerphone and his booming voice was so scary it could have Navy SEAL's shitting themselves.

"What the *fuck*, Stacy?! What have you done? I spent thirty minutes straight answering calls from random numbers, and every single one of them said they found Gerard and were calling for their reward." Angry didn't even begin to describe how he sounded. It didn't matter that I wasn't the one he was yelling at, it still caused a shiver to wrack through my body. Not much rattled Stacy, but I still expected her to be shaken up by his tone.

Fuck. That big-ass smile on her face meant that not only was she not affected by his shouting, but she was enjoying it. I needed to get out of there, and I started plotting my escape while listening to her respond in the calmest, most patronizing tone. *Shit, shit, shit.* I just knew I was going to be dragged into this fight somehow.

"Well, you see, someone stole Gerard. Last I checked, stealing is a crime. Since the cops, aka you, wouldn't help me locate him, I had to take matters into my own hands, so I put up posters all over the city."

"Every word of that is bat shit crazy, but the more important question is *why* did you put *my* phone number on the fliers?"

"Well, again, stealing is a crime. You are the police. I thought it best they contact law enforcement to report the crime." The way she explained it to him made it so sound perfectly reasonable that she almost had me convinced. Her nonchalant approach to the whole thing undoubtedly pissed Chad off even more.

"I was in a meeting with my captain, Stacy! I have to answer my phone in case it's in relation to an actual crime. I tried to ignore it and he forced me to answer every time. He was only a couple feet away from me, and I do *not* want to know how many times he heard the word dildo coming from the other line. You are really going to pay for this." I could picture Chad in my head, seething, his face red and his body shaking with anger. He was a force to be reckoned with when he was that mad, but you would only ever see him lose his shit like that when Stacy was involved. Ironically, she was also the only one who could calm him down.

Stacy was trying really, really hard not to laugh, which only made it that much louder when the laughter finally burst out of her mouth. "Oh my gosh, that's so awesome," she said in between laughs. "Oh man, that's so embarrassing. I should totally get two points for this one instead of one. I couldn't have planned that better if I tried."

I could have sworn I actually *felt* Chad's growl through the phone.

"Stevens!" A very loud, very irritated voice shouted through the phone. "Yes, sir?" Chad replied to the other voice, his tone calm and professional. What the mystery voice said next had to have taken Chad from angry to murderous. "I found this flier in the hallway. Look familiar to you? I'm assuming this had something to do with all those calls you took during our meeting?"

"Oh shit!" Stacy yelled, clicking the 'end call' button on her phone, just before falling out of her chair. She was laughing so hard that she literally fell out of her chair and onto the floor. I couldn't hold it in any longer, so I gave up the fight and joined her in the laughter while helping her stand up.

"You are going to be in so much trouble when he gets home tonight, Stacy," I said shaking my head, still laughing. Stacy straightened out her clothes and responded to me with a look of pure evil.

"That's what I was counting on. Angry Chad is a

beast in bed. But enough about me, it's time for you to fess up about what's going on between you and Joe."

"To be honest, I'm not sure. Last night was...amazing. More than that, really, there's just no way to describe it. I've had sex plenty of times, but with Joe - and even without the orgasms - it was so much better. I didn't even know it could be like that, and it's probably because he's so experienced, but damn does he know how to move those hips. If he ever gives up law enforcement, he could take his cop uniform and work the pole."

"I could so picture Joe being a stripper. He would eat that shit up. He's such an attention whore." Stacy leveled a serious look my way, and I tossed back another shot, knowing that whatever she was about to say was going to require more alcohol. It was that look she gives as a warning before she fully inserts herself into your business in the most unwelcome of ways. "So what does this mean? Are you guys just hooking up? Are you exclusive? What's the deal?"

"Jesus, Stacy, I don't know. We didn't do much talking last night, and he was gone when I woke up."

"That asshole snuck out on you!?"

"Chill your panties, geez. He didn't sneak out, he left a note and even had flowers delivered early this morning."

"That's more like it. I know Joe isn't usually a stick around for morning canoodling kind of guy, even though it's well known that he enjoys a good cuddle. The morning after awkward shit is what he doesn't like, but I'd put money on it that you're the first one who's ever gotten flowers from him. And to my knowledge, he's always been totally upfront about his lack of interest in a relationship. Though, obviously it's different with you, so I doubt his usual M.O. is any use in this situation. So when are you going to see him again?"

I shrugged and tried not to let her see how disappointed I was that I hadn't heard from Joe yet today. I mean, yeah, he sent me flowers and it was sweet, but I was in unchartered territory and it was freaking me the shit out. Feeling insecure made me feel vulnerable, which made me want to run in the opposite direction.

All day I'd kept waiting for that fear to snake its way into my head and tell me to be rational, to not let Joe in, but it never happened. I still felt scared, but in a way that was much more manageable. I actually *wanted* to take the risk with Joe, and I'd never felt that way with a man. The persistent bastard had finally made his way past all my walls, and it seemed he wasn't going anywhere. Or would he stop trying so hard now that he'd finally gotten me into bed? *Shit.* No, he sent me flowers, that had to be a good sign.

I could have lived my whole life without hearing that little tidbit about Joe being a cuddler. The less I knew about his past, the better. There wasn't a chance in hell I could compare to those other women in bed, but I sure as fuck wasn't going to start comparing myself to them, either. If his past conquests were anything like the bitch at the coffee shop, then they couldn't hold a candle to me in any other sense.

Her little remark about being the only one Joe ever slept with regularly popped into my head. I hadn't given her any thought since then, but that was before I'd seen him naked. I couldn't imagine going the rest of my life without getting to see that body. Just thinking about it had me wanting to shove my hand in my pants right there at Stacy's kitchen table. How on earth would I be able to go forever without getting to actually touch it again?

No, I couldn't do that. I couldn't imagine going more than a day without getting to run my tongue over his skin, starting with his chest, moving down his stomach and following the lines of his abs to that beautiful V that points straight to the most delicious dick I'd ever tasted.

"Earth to Carrie," Stacy snapped her fingers in my face. "Stop having imaginary sex in my kitchen and answer my freaking question."

"Um, wh-what was it? Your question?"

"Oh Lord. If just one night of orgasms has got you this flighty, then I hate to see what you'll be like in a few days."

"Screw you. And I don't know. I haven't heard from

him." I didn't look at her, but I could feel her annoyance. "Oh my gosh, what?"

"I think this is one of those times when the girl should actually reach out to the guy. You've been playing hard to get for months, so I don't think it would hurt for you to put yourself out there a little."

I knew Joe cared about me in a way that went beyond lust, but that didn't mean he wanted to keep me in his bed long term. Just because he had friendly feelings toward me - that for all I knew, had more to do with Stacy than me - didn't mean we were going to start some kind of relationship. It was this exact type of situation that had always kept me from sleeping with guys I knew. Not to say my hookups were with strangers, but I always made sure I didn't have a connection to the men who warmed my bed.

It was an unorthodox way of doing things, and Stacy took a lot of opportunities to remind me how ridiculous she thought it was, but it had been working for me. I'd go on one date, and if I felt anything at all towards him, I would either plant his ass in the friend zone or just never see him again. However, if I found myself completely uninterested in ever seeing said man again, then I'd be putting out on the first date.

It wasn't something I practiced often, and the number of guys I'd been with was a modest amount. My therapist was wholly against my dating policies, but since she hadn't been able to offer me a sound alternative, I'd kept with it.

Until Joe. I hadn't dated, *truly dated*, since Brad. I hadn't even had the desire to see someone regularly, so it wasn't like I was denying myself anything. Unlike Joe, I didn't stay the night and do the cuddling bit, so he was the first man to stay over in my bed. I'd woken up in the middle of the night and had a quasi-panic attack when I felt a warm, hard body curled up behind me. I'd never been the little spoon. I'd never been *any* spoon. And it was how much I liked it that scared me. After turning in his arms, he gave me a gentle peck on the tip of my nose, without waking up. It had felt natural, like it was instinct for him to just kiss me. Like his body was telling him, even when unconscious, that he wanted me.

But no, that was too good to be true. It had nothing to do with me, because Joe was a damn *cuddler*. He probably kissed all the women he slept with on the nose in the middle of the night. They probably relished in being a spoon and didn't freak the hell out over it. Only Stacy was right, things with me were different. If for no other reason than the fact that we had mutual friends and if he was an asshole to me, it would make both our lives very difficult.

I had a sinking feeling that those flowers were a way to soften the blow, let me down easy. He'd done it, finally gotten me naked. Accomplished what no other man had ever done - brought me to orgasm and turned me into a...gag...cuddler. Of course, he didn't know the word cuddle was more disgusting to me than the word moist. He had no idea how big of a deal last night had been to me.

A very massive part of me wanted to tell him. To let him know how special it was, *he was*, to me. The part of me that dared to hope wanted to run to him and confess everything, even the parts I hadn't yet admitted to myself. That part - the part that hoped - was getting bigger by the day. Consuming the rest of me, turning me into one of those girls who draws her boyfriend's name inside of a heart and practices her signature while planning their wedding before ever getting a ring.

I always hated romantic movies and chick flicks for that reason. Girls sat around acting foolish and giving the man all the power, just waiting on their asses for him to realize he's in love. I'd vowed to never be one of them. I had too much self respect to sit around plucking petals off flowers or go skipping around like a freaking Disney princess.

Yet, there I was, letting that damn hope get to me. Letting the doubt and insecurities that accompany that hope eat at me, until I was questioning everything. Like how could someone as inexperienced as me keep Joe interested, in or out of the bedroom? Neither of us had any experience when it came to relationships, so surely we would be destined to crash and burn, right? What if I finally let him in and I screwed things up? Or worse, he just abandoned me like my dad did?

It was a bullshit way to spend my time, going over all the what-ifs. I'd never really been a jealous person when it came to men, probably because I'd never cared about anyone enough to feel jealousy. On top of all the other shit that threatened to stand in the way of making something with Joe - something that really mattered - I also had competition. Enough competition to fill a small arena, and going by what that skank that ambushed me in the coffee shop said, a good number of them were probably insane.

Stacy had told me that the women Joe slept with always knew the score, that it wasn't anything but sex, but I'd be willing to bet money that several - if not all of them - hoped it would end up being more. What girl wouldn't want to be the one who finally got a catch like Joe to settle down? If skank-face had taught me anything, it was that I was kidding myself if I thought the numerous women he'd been with weren't going down without a fight.

Did I want to be the one to pull someone with such a high demand off the market? I could already picture the claw marks on my face. And maybe I was being dramatic, but it's not like I had a reference point to go off of. My hatred for romance movies also extended to books, television and anything else that might have given me some inkling as to how I should proceed. Not that any of that shit was realistic, anyway. All the advice in the world wouldn't change the fact that if I decided to really give it a go with him, it wasn't going to be easy.

"Hellooooo," Stacy drawled out impatiently. "I don't know where you keeping going, but before you disappear again, let me get something out." *Internal eye roll.* "Be careful."

"I know you're worried about me, Stace, but-"

"No, I'm not worried about you getting hurt. I'm worried about you hurting Joe."

What the fuck? "Excu-"

"Hang on, don't get all pissy-pants on me. Hear me out. Joe has never had a real relationship, but not because he's a commitment-phobe, he just never found a woman worth taking a risk on. He picked you, Lord help him, and I know him well enough to know that he's fully invested in this. So if any part of you doesn't want this, be honest with him, because he deserves to know the truth. Don't break his heart, Care."

Well, shit.

CHAPTER 12
JOE

Three days. Three damn days and no word from Carrie. During those three days, in which I'd incessantly checked my phone about a thousand times a day, I'd also come to the conclusion that I must have grown a pussy because I sure as hell had been thinking like one.

Giving Carrie her first sex-induced orgasm had me strutting around with my chest puffed all the next day, but with each day that passed and I didn't hear from her, it slowly started to deflate.

Climbing out of her bed that morning was so damn hard. Seeing her laying in bed with her hair splayed across her pillow, the light streaming through the window made her brown hair look like it had specs of gold scattered throughout it. Her soft, pink lips parted just enough to remind me of what they felt like wrapped around my cock. She looked so small on her massive bed, her delicate fingers curled up beneath her head. All I wanted was to climb back into bed with her and relive the past night's events over and over again until neither of us could walk.

There wasn't time. I had to work the early shift and was already running late. Staying over had not been the plan, and I was too busy ravishing every inch of her to remember to set an alarm. I contemplated waking her up, not wanting her to think I was being a dick and skipping out on her, but she looked too peaceful. I stood there and stared at her for so long that it was bordering on creepy, but every time I tried to walk away, I couldn't get my legs to move.

I was already ordering the flowers before I'd made it to my car. I wanted to do something that would show her what was going on between us was real. That I wasn't avoiding her by leaving before she woke. That I was still thinking about her, even hours later.

I'd never sent a girl flowers. It's not like I expected her to flip out or anything, but a damn 'thank you' text would have been nice. I had no idea what to think, not a clue about what was going on with her. Did she regret it? I couldn't imagine that would be possible, because I'd made damn sure that it had been as enjoyable for her as it was for me.

I wanted to declare my intentions, make sure she understood that it wasn't a one-time thing for me. I knew my reputation bothered her. She'd never come right out and said so, but she'd eluded to it enough times for me to know it was on her mind a lot. I hated knowing she probably thought she was one of many, that she would get the same deal as all the others.

I couldn't even fathom wanting someone else any-more. She was all I wanted, all I thought about. And that was *before* the mind blowing sex. I wasn't anywhere close to being as much of a man slut as people gave me credit for, but I'd had enough sex to know that what happened between me and Carrie wasn't your average, everyday, run of the mill roll in the sack.

I'd never felt so connected, so intensely in the moment as I did with her. My thoughts didn't stray from her, and no matter how many times we brought each other to orgasm, my need for her never diminished. If anything, it became more intense. I thought for sure she was feeling it too. So why hadn't I heard from her?

"Hey, Joe. Can I ask you a personal question?"

I knew I'd been unusually quiet for our shift, too lost in my thoughts to really engage, but Chad *never* asked me personal questions. The shock of him asking permission to do so had me snapping back into the present so fast I ended up swerving the squad car into the wrong lane.

"Shit!" I gripped the steering wheel, veering us to the right lane. "Sorry. Yeah, buddy. Go right ahead."

"I've just noticed something lately, and as your friend and partner, I feel obligated to address it with you."

Chad was being way too serious, which meant either something was really bothering him or he was fucking with me. It was most likely the latter, but I was grateful for any distraction, even if it came at my expense. So

I took the bait and nodded for him to go on.

"I was wondering what happened to your balls."

I yanked on the wheel - that time intentionally - and pulled the cruiser over to the side of the road. When I punched him in his fucking face I didn't want to die in a fiery inferno as a result by wrecking the fucking car.

"Are they lost? Defective? Maybe they just quit working. Or did you loan them out and never get them back? Let me know, and I'll help you buddy. Don't worry, we'll get your manhood back. That's what friends are for."

He put a sympathetic hand on my shoulder, trying and failing to hide his grin. I smacked his arm off my shoulder and glared at him.

"You're an asshole."

"I've been called worse."

I considered actually punching him for a second, but who the fuck was I kidding? He was right. I'd had those same exact thoughts over and over again every time I checked my phone or deleted another text I had spent too much time typing but was too chicken shit to send. I put the car in motion again and pretended to be pissed off. He was just giving me shit, but if he knew I actually agreed with him then I'd never live it down. "Whatever dude. You're so pussy whipped by Stacy, you have no room to talk. Since you guys finally got your shit together, I hardly ever see her."

"Aw, I'm sorry. Am I getting in the way of your girl bonding time?"

A call came through before I could respond. A minor dispute among patrons at a strip club nearby. I quickly took the call, thankful for anything to avoid the ribbing Chad was giving me. I didn't mind him giving me shit, but I wasn't in the mood when I had no idea what was going on between Carrie and me to begin with.

It only took us minutes to make the trek to The Yellow Brick Road with the lights on. I'd never been inside the strip club personally, but from what I'd heard it was a pretty decent one. I'd actually only ever been inside a strip club once for a bachelor party, and I wasn't impressed, so I'd never felt the need to see another.

One foot inside the door and I could tell this joint was nothing like the one I'd been to previously. It was Wizard of Oz themed, hence the name, and all the girls were in character. Very scantily clad version of the movie, mind you, but it worked. Other than some modern art that paid tribute to the movie, the rest of the place was pretty simple. Nothing gaudy or over the top, but rather a pretty laid back atmosphere.

A man who looked to be a manager greeted us as soon as we walked in, leading us over to the two men who'd been the reason for the call. It couldn't have been too bad of a fight, because neither seemed injured and they hadn't been kicked out. Instead they were seated at tables across from each other, both with a burly and menacing looking bouncer next to them, while they glared daggers at each other.

"Our guys jumped in before things escalated, and both these men are regulars who we've not had any prior issues with. We didn't want to make a big scene or ban them, but we felt we should still call the authorities on the chance it ever happens again. Should things have gotten violent before we could intervene, then we would have had no choice but to press charges."

The manager went on to explain the misunderstanding between the men, which boiled down to which one got a lap dance from a popular dancer first. Petulant man-children fighting over a woman they paid to dance for them? Pathetic, in my opinion. Still, we did our job and gave them a 'stern talking to' as if they were kids narrowly escaping a trip to juvie.

"Son of a bitch," Chad muttered under his breath as we headed for the door after wrapping up. Before I could ask him what he was bitching about he was sprinting for the door.

"Stop right there!"

I'd know that scary, high-pitched yell anywhere. *Carrie.*

"Nope! Shift's over. Find your own way back, Joe. C-ya!"

I was still too fucking stunned to see Carrie in a strip

club to worry about Chad running out of there like a little pussy. *Asshole*.

"Why hello there, half pint. Fancy seeing you here." Flashes of her naked, writhing body underneath mine while she cried out my name were going off at rapid fire. I couldn't have stopped my gaze from going lower if my life depended on it. Even when she coughed, trying to get my eyes to break away from her chest, I remained glued. I knew what was beneath that little blouse she was wearing. Knew what it felt like, tasted like, and how it puckered with the flick of my tongue.

She pushed me, which did the trick. The lights were dim, but not dark enough to keep me from seeing the fire in her eyes. The angry kind, not the wanna-get-naked-with-you kind.

"What the hell are you doing here?"

"Whoa. I was responding to a call. Why are you snapping at me?" She sighed and looked around for a few seconds before grabbing my hand and pulling me to a booth in the corner.

"*Fuck*. Okay, shit's gonna hit the fan now anyway, so whatever." I couldn't tell if she was talking to me or mumbling to herself. "Go ahead, ask."

"Why are *you* here?"

"This is my strip club." If she hadn't said it so matter-of-factly, I would have thought I misheard her.

"Say what?"

"I own it." She said those three words like they explained everything. I waited with an eyebrow quirked, letting her know I would wait all day. She wasn't getting off that easy. "After shit went down with Brad, I was feeling bad about myself. I was searching for something, I didn't know what, but one of my dancers had been a stripper here while putting herself through college. The way she talked about it, like it was freeing and empowering...it sounded like it was exactly what I needed. So I auditioned and was hired. I worked here two nights a week for about a year before I bought it."

What the holy of mother shit…

"You...you were a *stripper*?"

Her nose scrunched up adorably. "Don't say it like it's a dirty word. These girls work hard and are extremely talented. They aren't hookers, they're entertainers. And yes, I was until I bought the place. The previous owner was getting up there in age and was just going to close it down, and I couldn't let all the girls lose their jobs. Business was slow but it just needed a makeover and some rebranding. Luckily, I have a brother who owns a very successful business specializing in that very thing. I had to dump a load of money into it at first to get it where it needed to be, but I earned it back within the first year."

She talked about it like it was just a normal, everyday business transaction. This small, mostly quiet, puzzling woman owned a strip club. The woman who was dressed like a soccer mom on her way to a parent-teacher conference the first time I met her used to be a stripper.

I just needed a minute to let that digest.

"How...why...this seems like something that would come up at some point. Why did I not know about it until now?"

She shrugged. Fucking *shrugged*. "Stacy sucks at keeping secrets, but this is one she managed to shut up about. I think mostly because Ian would lose his shit if he found out I used to be a stripper. He's a little over-protective, especially when it comes to me, but mostly it would hurt his feelings that I did this without him. He would have wanted to give advice and get his lawyers involved and crap, and I wanted this to be my own thing."

"Even without Stacy telling him, you'd think he would have found out by now? Seems like a pretty big secret."

Again with the shrugging. "I'm a silent partner, so my name isn't on any documents that are easy to find. I didn't do any personal lap dances or anything, I just performed on stage, so no one really got close enough to me to see who I was. It's not something I've gone out of my way to keep from him, so if he found out it wouldn't be the end of the world. Which I'm sure he will now, since you and Chad know, but it was bound to happen eventually. So, whatever."

She was being so freaking blasé about it all. Every time I blinked my eyes she threw a curveball at me. *Would I ever truly know this woman?*

I sat back, crossed my arms and looked at her. *Really* looked at her. It was laughable, looking back on how I used to think of her. Assuming she was a timid, mousy little woman. Stacy was definitely right. Carrie had layers. Layers wrapped around layers, and damn it was going to be fun peeling them all away. I knew what was in the juicy center. It was worth the work.

"Such a shame," I said with a sigh, shaking my head. I waited for her to get that defensive, angry look in her eye before I continued. "I would have loved to see you do your thing, but since you're retired I'll never get the chance. It's extremely disappointing."

I was growing to love all versions of Carrie, but the competitive I'll-show-you Carrie was quickly becoming my favorite. She rose to her feet and leaned over the table, putting her face inches away from mine.

"Run home and change out of your uniform, pretty boy. Be back here in thirty minutes and I'll make all your dreams come true." Oh, shit. Her voice was a seductive whisper, and I was getting hard just from her words. I'd probably blow a load in my pants when she actually got up on stage. I adjusted myself before standing, intentionally being obvious about it. I *wanted* her to know how much she affected me.

She smirked as she walked away, her ass swaying

in a way that made it impossible for me to not reach out and grab a feel. She didn't smack my hand away or tell me to keep my hands to myself. She just winked over her shoulder before disappearing backstage.

Fuck, it was going to be a good day.

CHAPTER 13
CARRIE

Once I was backstage I had to lean on a wall to keep from crumbling. I'd been putting off talking to Joe, making one excuse after another, too afraid to face what I was feeling. That man in his uniform did stuff to me that had me acting like an entirely different person.

Example? Well, I had just agreed to get on stage and strip, so ya know...not something I would usually do spur of the moment. I was surprisingly nervous, but only because Joe did that to me. Getting on stage, even half naked, didn't bother me. And even though Joe had seen every bare inch of my body - even places I couldn't see myself - didn't do a damn thing to make it any easier to strip in front of him.

There was no possible way he could go home and back in thirty minutes. He lived at least forty minutes from the club. That gave me plenty of time to figure out a way out of this.

I peeked out of the door leading to the dressing area to see how busy the club was, and my jaw hit the floor when I saw Joe sitting at a table front and center. *What the hell?* It had only been twenty minutes, and he didn't even have a car. Chad had ditched him. Where did he get clothes?

My phone buzzed in my pocket. *Fucking Stacy*.

Got a surprising text from Joe asking me to bring him a change of clothes at a little strip club nearby. Lucky for him I had nothing to do. Lucky for me, I finally get to see my bestie dance.

I was going to kill her.

"Thanks for loaning me your Glenda costume, Tay," I thanked one of the other dancers after I got off stage. I was changing back into my regular clothes when Stacy came barging in.

"You can't be back here, Stace." She knew that. She also never listened. I had to kick her out more often than the bouncers had to kick out handsy drunks. She was incorrigible.

"That was some performance, Care. You even got me feeling a little hot after that."

"You are always horny, Stacy. Vegetables are a turn on for you."

"Well so many of them are phallic shaped! It's not *my* fault that my mind automatically starts thinking about penises when I see them!"

Stacy said she was taking off, and I took my time cleaning up before heading back out to face Joe. It seemed I'd taken too long and someone had beaten me to him, because when I emerged I was greeted with the sight of one of the dancers talking to Joe. She had that look in her eye. The same one I'm sure I always had when I was talking to him. It made me want to smack her. I didn't just get up on stage and strut my naked ass off for him so that some other girl could flirt with him. *Hells no.*

I hadn't met her. I didn't know all the dancers, I wasn't involved in much of the day to day operations anymore. That meant she didn't know who I was, which also meant she didn't know her job was on the line when she looked at me like I was shit on her shoe as I walked up.

"Hey sweetie," I said as I kissed Joe on the cheek. If my affections shocked him, he didn't show it.

"Hey beautiful," he said back as he kissed me square on the mouth. It wasn't a particularly sexual kiss, but it wasn't a chaste, friendly kiss either. He snaked his arm around my shoulder and squeezed me into his side, but little miss fake-boobs in her slutty Dorothy outfit wasn't phased. I picked out that outfit, but it looked trashy on her.

Ugh, I was being so juvenile.

When she ran a finger down his chest, all guilt I felt about my bitchy thinking flew right out the fucking window. Joe politely pushed her hand away and took a step back, pulling me with him. She didn't take the hint, and instead took two steps forward, putting her body almost flesh with his. He still had his arm around me, holding me snug to his side, and she *still* continued to paw him.

We did that little dance a few more times before I lost it.

"Um, hellooo?" I waved my hand in front of the blonde bimbo's face dramatically to get her attention. "You see me standing here?" She looked at me like I'd lost my mind, and maybe I had, but I wasn't going to stand idly by while some bitch hit on Joe with me standing right next to him.

"Actually, I hadn't noticed you until you put your obnoxious little hand in my face," she said snottily.

"Yeah, well, maybe you should try looking with your eyes and not your vagina next time, because this man standing next to me that you keep trying to paw with your slutty mitts? He's mine, and hitting on him with his girlfriend standing right fucking next to him is kind of rude."

Joe snickered next to me, and I knew very well that I was acting like a jealous twat, but I didn't really give a shit at the moment. I had just bared myself to him, literally, so I wasn't going to just sit idly by while some whore tried to flirt with him. He didn't know it yet, but I'd decided I really wanted to give things a shot with him, but putting up with slutty silicone sexpots was not going to be part of the deal.

Joe seemed unphased by her pathetic attempts to flirt

with him, though he had tensed up when she finally addressed me specifically with her snotty little remark. Part of me braced myself for Joe to step in and diffuse the situation. I had no claim to him. I hadn't even thanked him for sending me flowers. It was a pretty bold move to tell another woman to bugger off when I was ignoring him.

I knew Joe was a really nice guy, and I was being anything but nice the majority of the time. He never seemed to get worked up about anything, whereas I was practically a freaking pro at making a scene. I wasn't as bad as Stacy, but I wasn't one to shy away from confrontation either.

Subconsciously I was aware that this unexpected scenario had turned into a test of sorts. If Joe stepped in and tried to excuse her behavior or apologize to her on my behalf - which happened with Brad too many times to count - then I'd know a relationship wasn't in the cards for us. Every time Brad acted embarrassed when I stood up for myself it made me feel small, like my feelings were insignificant. He never had my back, and I wasn't going to keep my mouth shut just to keep someone else happy.

I wasn't going to come second to another woman, for any reason, especially when it was someone just trying to get in his pants.

"Aw, that's so cute that you think you're Joe's girlfriend," she said condescendingly before turning her attention to Joe. "I'm a little surprised at you, though. You normally tell the girls the score up front. Not like you to lead one on."

She was acting so smug, with her taunting smile and cocky stance. It made me wish I had real claws so I could tear up her pretty little face.

I stepped out of Joe's hold and opened my mouth to lay into her again, but stopped when I felt Joe's arm go around my waist, pulling me back to him. His other arm wrapped around me in a hug, my back to his front, and he placed a gentle kiss on the top of my head. BitchTits reared back at the affectionate display like someone had slapped her, which wasn't as gratifying as actually getting to slap her, but still felt pretty good.

"Actually, Carrie *is* my girlfriend, and I don't appreciate you speaking to her the way you are. And you're right, I always let them know the score and I've never been a monogamous kind of guy, but that's only because I hadn't found someone worth it before. Now that I have, I have no intention of letting her go. So from here on out I would appreciate it if you treated Carrie with the respect she deserves."

I had to school my expression because I did not want her to see the shocked reaction I was actually feeling. Yeah, I knew Joe was attracted to me and had some affectionate-type feelings towards me, but it's not like we'd made any declarations of love. Hell, I'd acted like a bitch by ignoring him the last few days. The totally calm and polite way he explained that I'm not going anywhere? It did things to my insides that had me wanting to go all fan girl on him right there on the spot.

"Trina's not going to be happy about this." I was looking back at Joe and it didn't even register what she had said until I watched Joe's face morph from adoring as he looked at me, to full on rage when he looked back at the little home wrecker. I'd never seen him so angry, and my body instinctively tried to pull away, but he kept his arm wound tightly around me.

"I don't give a flying fuck how Trina feels. My personal life is none of her damn business, despite how much she inserts herself into it. So you run along and tell Trina and all her cronies that none of you are to come within ten feet of Carrie, or me, if you plan to cause any unnecessary drama."

We both watched as the bitch retreated with a huff, walking like a girl on a mission, which I had no doubt meant she was headed off to talk to this "Trina" person.

I looked up at Joe, noticing a tenseness in him that looked so odd on his normally relaxed face. Easy-going, smooth talking, charm-your-pants-off Joe was a lady killer, for sure. But this no-nonsense, take charge, intimidating Joe was so sexy that I felt my lady parts getting all warm and tingly.

I debated bending over right there, giving him an

obvious invitation to take me in front of whoever chose to look, but he looked down at me before I had a chance to follow through on that ridiculously impulsive move. Immediately the hard lines were gone as he gazed down at me, and the warmth in his eyes made my lady parts go from tingly to all out buzzing like they'd been electrocuted.

"Girlfriend, huh?" His mouth tilting up to form that cocky smirk he wore so well had me staring at him like a fool, uncomprehending what he was saying.

"Huh?" I asked dumbly, before it hit me what he'd said. "Shit, oh my gosh. I did say that, didn't I? I'm so sorry, I don't know what came over me. Heat of the moment and all that. I mean, we haven't even gone on a date and I never thanked you for the flowers. Thank you, by the way. I'm sorry I haven't called or texted you. It's been...I had a lot to figure out and I didn't want to screw things up. I suck at this, if you can't tell by now, and I just kind of flipped when I saw her flirting with you. Once I worked up the courage I was going to call you and tell you that I wanted to try this out, see if you maybe wanted to, I don't know, go out? Does that sound lame? I don't know what the hell I'm talking about. I'm sure you don't-"

His tender lips on mine shut me up in the sweetest of ways, thank God, because my nervous rambling was getting worse and worse by the second. And if I'd had any doubt as to whether or not he wanted this too, the way he kissed me made it clear that he planned to keep me, at least for a while.

Every time he kissed me, somehow it got better, and I wondered at what point the newness of it all would wear off. And the fear of it wearing off for him sooner than me was definitely an underlying insecurity of mine, but it was hard to worry about that when his mouth was worshiping me in the way only someone who really cared about you could.

When we finally broke apart, my lips chased his, not wanting the moment to end. Then I realized I was leaning forward with my eyes closed and lips puckered like some kind of idiot, so I snapped to attention and looked around me. We didn't have an audience, so my nerves died down a bit.

"In case you couldn't tell, you have nothing to worry about. I decided you were mine a long time ago; I was just waiting for you to catch up. I don't want anyone else, just you. So you most definitely *are* my girlfriend, and you have no idea what it did to me, hearing you say it. Jealous little thing, though, aren't you?"

Take the plunge, Carrie. All in.

"I didn't used to be, but I am with you apparently. I'm like a woman possessed. But before we do this, like...go all in...I have some conditions." It was shitty timing, I knew that. It was also a necessary evil before

I took the plunge. Joe didn't seem to mind. His smile never faltered. In fact, it lit up a little more with a hint of amusement. "I don't have a list or anything, so these conditions will pop up as we go. We're both novices at relationships, so you know...learning curve. But you should know now, that if another bimbo pulls that crap I will react the same damn way. If it bothers you that I get jealous or territorial then say so now, because I don't even know if I can control it when it comes to you."

Joe seemed to ponder that for a moment, his brow furrowing. *Shit.*

"Okay, let me ask you this." He brushed a piece of my hair behind my ear gently, and I let out a dreamy sigh, like some kind of boy crazy little nitwit. "Your jealousy...is it because you're afraid you can't trust me?"

Fuck all, but every time Joe showed me a little bit of his vulnerable side I fell just a little more for him.

"No, I can't even really explain it. At least not without sounding like a needy hag of a girlfriend." *Girlfriend.* Even third graders had girlfriends. It shouldn't have affected me the way it did to say it out loud, but my heart pitter-pattered anyway.

He just stood there, so I knew he wasn't going to let me get off without spilling it. "Gah! Fine. I just...I don't want women even *thinking* that they have a chance with you. You're mine, and I'm sorry if that's like, reverse caveman type logic, but if you're my boyfriend then dammit, I own you. I don't want them all flirty and crap, thinking it makes a difference, especially when I'm right there. It's seriously rude, like...way more rude than half the crap I do, which is saying a lot. And I'm no doormat, so I'm not going to let people treat me like one just to keep from making you or anyone else uncomfortable. If I don't like their behavior, I'm going to say so."

Without hesitation, Joe planted a chaste kiss on my lips and stated, "I love you just the way you are. I wouldn't ask you to change."

Holy what the what? I seriously would have thought I misheard him if his own jaw hadn't fallen open at his admission. We stared at each other in stunned silence, and I couldn't tell if the fear in his eyes was because he hadn't meant to admit how he really felt, or if it just came out the wrong way and he was afraid I was going to be upset if he didn't really mean it.

An absurd amount of time passed with neither of us speaking, and I felt a nervous bubble of laughter sneaking up my throat. I let it free, bending over hysterically and causing a scene. It was quite the scene, me wheezing and laughing so hard I had tears streaking down my face. My cheeks hurt and my stomach muscles contracted over and over again, and out of the corner of my eye I saw Joe joining in.

Finally, when I slowed down enough to talk, I assured him I understood what he meant and it was no big deal. I teased him relentlessly the whole drive back to my apartment, and while the hysterics were real, the casualness of it all was not.

I was telling him different, but Joe had just freaked me the fuck out.

JOE

The days following my Freudian slip, things were surprisingly normal. I kept waiting for Carrie to freak out or get weird, but the more time that went by without that happening, the more I started to relax.

It wasn't that I hadn't meant to say it out loud, it was that I hadn't meant to say it at all. Mostly because until that very moment, I didn't even know it was true. But it was. *I loved her.*

I also felt regret over my history for the first time in my life. I wasn't the manwhore everyone made me out to be, but I was a relentless flirt. My never bothering to correct anyone's assumptions had Carrie doubting my ability to stay faithful to her. I understood it, didn't take it personally. I also really wanted her to trust me and let me in, which I couldn't see happening until she knew without a doubt that I only had eyes for her.

Love? *Shit.* I was terrified to be in love with her, but not for any of the reasons a man is normally terrified when it comes to relationships. It was how much of a flight risk she was. I always felt like I was walking on eggshells, tiptoeing around and second guessing everything I said and did. It didn't make me resent her, and I didn't mind the work, but it did make me feel like there was still a gaping hole between us.

Approaching the subject with her would be risky at best, so I figured toughing it out a while longer was the best option. See if over time she might come to realize I wasn't going anywhere, and maybe eventually she would completely let me in. The only problem was that until that happened, I would still have the nagging fear that she might up and change her mind.

So yeah, knowing that I was fucking in love with her? Scary shit.

I wasn't going to do something stupid, like push her away or sabotage myself or anything just because I was afraid, but I needed some time to think. Get my head on straight before I did something equally stupid, like go shopping for engagement rings or something. I was completely out of my element, and I knew how I handled things next was crucial to how my future would play out with Carrie.

My house was the last place I'd be able to find refuge. I used to love always having people in my house, knowing I'd never be alone. After what happened to my parents, the thought of being alone in my house made me physically ill. But the more time I spent with Carrie, the less my past haunted me, and the more I wanted the never-ending parties to stop.

Somehow I ended up at Chad's, most likely my masochistic subconscious looking for ways to inflict pain on myself. The sad truth was that Chad and Stacy were my only real friends, despite how many visitors I always had. The saddest part of that sad truth was even though I knew they would help me with my problem, they would also give me shit about it, probably for the rest of my life. If it weren't for the direness of it all, I would have just avoided talking to them about it altogether.

They didn't exactly have the healthiest of relationships, even though they had come a long way since their early dysfunctional days, but they were the only people I knew in a serious relationship. Well, there was Ian and Adalyn, but I wasn't all that close to them. Not close enough to go seeking relationship advice, anyway.

Who would have thought I'd ever be seeking out relationship advice?

I almost turned around and left when I approached their door and heard a crash and then the sound of glass breaking, followed by Stacy shrieking, but there was a good chance that even if I tried again another day the outcome would still be the same.

After at least five minutes of knocking, a very winded Stacy answered the door. Her mischievous smile was contagious, and for a second I forgot the reason I'd stopped by to begin with. One of the reasons I loved Stacy - she could make you forget your shit with the snap of a finger. Without saying a word, Stacy grabbed my wrist and yanked me inside, then hid behind me like she was ducking for cover.

"What the-"

"Stacy!" Chad's angry voice boomed from down the hall, and Stacy's giggling guaranteed a very disgruntled man was going to be charging into the room any second. "What the fuck do you...oh, hey Joe. When did you get here?"

Chad went from furious to friendly in two-point-oh seconds flat, but Stacy jumped out from behind me and Chad immediately morphed back into an angry beast.

"Cease fire! Cease fire!"

Stacy was holding her hands in the air, a gesture of surrender, with a handheld gun in her right hand. She slowly lowered it, the way we instruct perps to when we are making them surrender their weapons before getting arrested. After it hit the ground, she kicked it towards Chad with the toe of her shoe and took a step back, her hands still in the air.

It was then that I noticed Chad's shirt was soaking wet, and the gun Stacy had laid on the ground was a toy squirt gun. Laughter burst out of me, and damn it felt good to let the stress go for a few minutes. Not that my situation with Carrie was making me miserable, but the whole not knowing what to do about it part was.

"Alright, truce," Chad said solemnly. If I didn't know better, I'd think he was actually enjoying his little water gun fight with Stacy. Then again, if anyone could get him to let loose and goof off, Stacy would be the one. "So, lady troubles, eh?" Chad said with a slap on my back as he walked past me to take a seat on the couch.

"What the-how did you know why I was here?" Chad had been unusually perceptive lately, and I was sure Stacy was to blame. For years I'd wanted my partner to open up and actually talk to me, but little did I know that he was an annoying little fucker when he did.

Chad shot me an incredulous look before taking a beer from Stacy. Stacy stretched her arm out to me, and I took the other one she was holding, then made myself comfortable. If they were going to give me shit about Carrie, then I was happy to drink all their beer and kick back while they had at it.

"So, Carrie still giving you a run for your money?"

Stacy's question surprised, and discouraged, me. I took a swig of my beer before responding.

"Apparently, since she didn't even deem me worthy of a little girl talk."

"Oh my gosh, Chad was right. You are so pussy whipped. Look at you, over there pouting like a little girl. What's up the with insecurity, Joe? This isn't like you."

"Shit, no one knows that better than me. I don't think I've been myself since the first night I met Carrie."

Chad grunted an agreement before leaning forward, putting his elbows to his knees and eyeing me carefully. "I'm gonna take a shot in the dark here, and you tell me if I got it right. She's got you questioning everything, probably even your own sanity. Making you wonder what the hell you're doing and not having a clue what you're *supposed* to do. You're probably feeling a little sick to your stomach and anxious enough with pent up energy that you could run a marathon. Am I close?"

"Yeah, that pretty much sums it up."

"So you love her, then?"

"How the hell did you become so astute, Chad? What the fuck has happened to you?"

Stacy snorted and took a drink of her own beer. "He's just as pussy whipped as you, that's what happened to him."

I looked to Chad, but he didn't even try to defend himself. Instead he gave her a sickeningly sweet smile, that from anyone else would actually have been a little moving, but coming from my partner who up until several months ago I was pretty sure didn't even actually have a heart, it was just awkward.

"Alright, so the jig is up and you know I'm in love. Now tell me what the hell to do so I don't screw up."

A moment of silence, then several moments of hysterical laughter.

"Glad my problems are so freaking entertaining to you two assholes," I muttered.

Stacy threw a pillow at my head right as I was taking a beer, causing it to splash up and out, soaking my shirt.

"There's nothing either of us can tell you that will keep you from screwing up. You are going to screw up, that's the only thing I know for sure. The question is, how are you going to handle it when you do? It's not avoiding the screw ups that makes a relationship last, it's knowing how to fix them."

"That's surprisingly great advice, Stacy." She threw another pillow at me, but I saw it coming and was able to dodge it. "So what you're telling me is, there's no way of knowing what will happen, other than the inevitability of my screwing up." Stacy nodded, and I mulled that over for a second.

"Okay, I can accept that there are no guarantees when it comes to relationships, but you know her better than I do, Stacy. So it should be no surprise to you when I say Carrie isn't your average girl, and hanging on to her is going to be more difficult than normal. Am I right?"

"Alright, enough girl talk for me. I'm out. Let me know if you want to work out your problems like a man at the gym," Chad threw out before shutting the front door behind him before I could come up with a retort.

"Listen, I wish I could tell you the secret way to Carrie's heart, but I have no freaking clue. That girl is a walking contradiction. She oozes sex and sensuality, but tries to hide it every chance she gets. She has more confidence than me, believe it or not, but only when she lets her guard down. It's like she forces herself to feel insecure, which is the most ass backwards way of thinking, but that's Carrie for you. The only advice I can give you is to be persistent. She will push you away, she will freak out, she might even run. But she needs someone who is going to stick by her even through all her crazy bullshit, so if you can't be that guy, then throw in the towel now before anyone gets hurt."

All things I already knew, but hearing them solidified in my mind what I had to do.

"Thanks. I'll see myself out." I hopped up and practically sprinted for the front door. The only way to handle this was to go at it head on. It was going to scare the life out of her, push her away, give her a reason to run, but it didn't matter. I loved her, and she deserved to know. One way or another, she'd find a reason to try and get rid of me, and like hell was I just going to sit around and wait for it to happen.

No, the best course of action would be to just lay it all on the line, let the cards fall as they may, and then cross my fingers and hope it didn't cost me everything.

CHAPTER 14
CARRIE

I was admittedly proud of myself for keeping it together. Since Joe's slip of the tongue, he'd been overtly romantic and sweet. Each time he did something unexpected, I had to talk myself off the ledge. It was exhausting and I was starting to get on my own damn nerves, but Joe deserved to be appreciated for the nice things he did. So I came up with a way to figure out how to handle all the new relationship-y crap I knew nothing about. Basically, I took my initial reaction and then did the exact opposite. It seemed to be working like a charm.

Weeks passed and it got easier to accept the affection he was showering me with without having to overthink everything. I kept thinking that over time things would dwindle, his efforts would lessen, but they never did. The fact that he kept going above and beyond to show he cared about me, even after bedding me several times, was reassuring. My insecurities were vanishing, and I held out hope that eventually they would disappear altogether.

My confidence in general only tended to waver when it came to men or relationships, and for once in my life I was fighting to keep someone, not push them away. I deserved a freaking gold star for that kind of personal growth.

"Hey, Carrie! What are you doing here?" Lacy's voice rang out from somewhere behind me, but in Grind's low lighting, I didn't spot her until she came out from behind the bar and stepped under one of the dim flood lights.

"Oh, hey Lacy. I was dropping off some information for Reed. I don't have an appointment; I was just in the area. You know if she's in?"

"You just missed her actually, but I'd be happy to pass this along for you?" There was something not quite right with the smile she gave me as I handed her the papers, like something was bothering her, but I didn't really know her well enough to pry.

"Well, thanks. It was good seeing you," I said as I turned to leave, then stopped in my tracks when she yelled out my name.

"Hey, um, I know it's none of my business, but I just wanted to say I'm sorry to hear about you and Joe."

Lacy had always seemed to be a somewhat pleasant person, and she hadn't even attempted to flirt with Joe since that day in Grind when I first met her. None of that mattered. Her bitchy remark had me spinning on my heels and marching right up to her. She was runway model tall and towered over me, but I was scrappy, and I'd cut a bitch if needed.

"And what, exactly, is that supposed to mean?" It

was the nicest thing I could think to respond with, since calling her a bitch and punching her in the nose didn't seem like a good decision. I said it through gritted teeth, it was practically a growl, but she didn't cower or get defensive. She looked at me like she pitied me. *What the hell?*

"For what it's worth, I thought you guys were great together. Men are idiots, and I guess Joe is no exception. So anyway, next time you come in, drinks on me, kay?"

"Um, thanks? But I'm not sure what you're talking about."

Lacy looked at me quizzically, as if *I* were the one not making any sense.

"I'm sorry, I thought that...well, I mean, it's just...I um..."

I was quickly losing patience with her stuttering. "Spit it out, Lacy. What are you talking about?" She winced and blurted out her answer so fast I almost didn't understand it.

"HehookedupwithTrinalastnight."

After taking a few seconds to repeat her sentence in my head a few times to decipher it, it finally dawned on me. "Who the hell is Trina? And what are you talking about? Joe was with me last night."

"Trina is the girl who was with me at the coffee shop when we ran into each other a while back. And I know they hooked up, because I was with her."

She went on explaining, but I didn't hear her. I was too busy trying to remember what time Joe left my place the night before. It had been earlier than normal, which I had thought weird at the time but easily dismissed. I had no reason to think it was weird. I completely trusted him.

Without another word, I left Grind and a very flustered Lacy behind me. Joe was off work that day, so he could only be a handful of places. I glanced at my phone and my stomach clenched when I read a text he'd sent me while I was talking with Lacy.

Gonna have to take a rain check on dinner. Something came up and don't know how long I'll be. Make it up to you tomorrow.

I felt angry and, admittedly, a tinge worried. But I trusted Joe. Despite his reputation, he truly was a good guy, and I knew that if he wanted to sleep with someone else, he would break it off with me first. It just wasn't his nature to do something so dick-ish.

So my anger was directed at this Trina slut, who was obviously spreading rumors. I didn't know how to find her, but I figured one of the dozens of people constantly traipsing around Joe's house probably would - she seemed like a frequent flyer.

The whole drive to Joe's house I was mentally patting myself on the back. In the past it wouldn't have even been a question of Joe's fidelity. I would have just assumed the worst. And maybe my new outlook was only applicable to this one man, but it was still progress. A step in the right direction, and a big leap in proving to myself - and Joe - that I could do this.

I was surprised when I pulled into Joe's driveway and saw his truck. Maybe whatever had kept him tied up had to do with his house or something. The worry I'd been feeling, I realized, was about Joe's reaction.

Would he be as bothered by this as I was?

Would he confront Trina and tell her to get lost, or would he put my feelings about it aside and dismiss her actions?

Shrugging off my worry, determined to keep my faith in Joe in tact, I pushed open the front door. I started to call out to him, but his voice interrupted me before I could speak. It sounded like it was coming from down the hall, and as I followed his voice, I could tell it was coming from his bedroom. His location combined with what he was saying was getting me very close to the point of breaking.

"Trina, you have to stop this."

That slut.

"Joe, why are you fighting this?"

Dammit! It wasn't even a phone conversation. That slut was in his bedroom with him!

I was about to shove the door the rest of the way open and start scratching her eyeballs out, but something kept me glued in place. A niggling feeling somewhere deep inside that made me feel like I needed the confirmation that he was going to resist her. It was shitty and horrible of me, but when your heart is on the line, you can end up doing the most despicable of things.

"I'm not fighting anything, Trina. Whatever you think is, or was, going on between us has always been in your head. I never promised you more than sex."

A high pitched whine-slash-groan coming from Trina had me cringing. Her voice was as annoying as nails on a chalkboard.

"Then why did you keep coming back for more? I'm the only one you slept with regularly. All the other girls it was a one-time deal, except for me. That has to mean something."

I rolled my eyes, even though no one was around to see it. My boyfriend was such a slut.

"I'm sorry if I led you on, but that wasn't my intention. I thought you understood. If I had thought for one second that you felt this way, then I wouldn't have kept hooking up with you."

A resounding slap noise came next, and I had to bite back a laugh. Served the asshole right for sticking his dick in so many women. I was *so* not going to let him live this down.

"This is all because of that whore!"

Ugh, bitch - what a hypocrite.

"Don't call her that, and Carrie has nothing to do

with this. I wouldn't feel anything for you even if Carrie weren't in the picture."

Damn straight! You tell her!

"That's bullshit, and you know it." I could just picture her in my head with her arms crossed and her foot stomping on the ground like a toddler throwing a tantrum. "You've changed, Joe. You practically disappeared, and when you are around, you're zero fun." Her voice took on a begging sound, which I imagined meant her lower lip was protruding. "I miss you. We had so much fun together. Why does you being with Carrie mean our fun has to stop?"

Freaking home wrecker. I'd just about hit my limit of what I could stomach to hear, but Joe's next words kept me frozen in place.

"Because I love her! Carrie is everything to me. She's not some random woman who's helping me scratch an itch, okay? I plan to make my life with her, and I don't appreciate you trying to stir up problems. I'm going to say it for the last time, and so help me, you better get it through your head. I'm. Not. Interested."

I knew he loved me already. Somewhere deep down, I *knew* that. But hearing him say it, and say it so passionately... I felt like I was going to hyperventilate. The rustling of fabric and Joe yelling at Trina pulled me from my panic, and I'd finally had enough.

I burst through the doors, taking only a brief second to take in the situation. Both mouths were dropped in surprise, but Trina's quickly morphed into a smug grin. My gaze dropped down to where Joe was shoving a trench coat into Amber's arms, which did little to cover up her entirely nude body.

Not only was she a slut, but she was a cliché slut.

"Carrie, I can-"

I didn't let Joe finish. I stormed over, ripped the coat from both of their hands, and grabbed Trina by the roots of her hair. She was almost a foot taller than me, but I'd developed enough of an attitude over the years to compensate for my small size, so her kicking and scratching did little to help her escape my clutches.

I was moving fast, and I felt her wobble behind me and cry out in pain, but I didn't stop to look back. I let go of her hair when we got to the front door so I could yank it open.

"You crazy bitch! Who the hell-whoa!"

With one hand clutching her coat I was only able to give her a one-handed shove. It didn't matter, though, because she had apparently lost a shoe during the struggle and she was caught off guard enough when I pushed her that she toppled down his front steps. When she landed - naked ass sticking up in the air - onto Joe's front lawn, I tossed her jacket at her.

In my periphery I saw Joe holding out her shoe, so I chucked that at her too.

"Next time you show your face around here, I won't be so nice when I kick you out."

She was yelling something about pressing charges when I slammed the door, not caring in the least about whatever threats she was tossing at me. I swiped my hands together, as if to knock off dirt or dust after a job well done, and marched over to Joe.

I looked up at him, his face a mixture of amusement and fear, and then I gripped his face with both my hands and pulled his lips down to mine. It was a tender kiss, and when Joe tried to deepen it, I pulled back.

"Carrie, you believe that nothing happened, right?" The vulnerability in his eyes almost made me change my mind, but the second I threw that bitch out the door, I had decided what I needed to do.

I took Joe's hand in mine and walked him over to the couch. I knew he wasn't going to understand, but I hoped he would respect my wishes anyway.

"Yes, I do believe you." I said it with enough conviction that it was unquestionable whether or not I meant it. Hearing that I believed him seemed to shock him more than relieve him. "I overheard more than I should have, and I'm sorry for eavesdropping. But I also want you to know that even if I hadn't, I would still believe you. I was actually on my way here to try and track her down."

"What? Why?"

"I was at Grind earlier, and Lacy gave me her condolences for our relationship. Apparently she's under the impression that you hooked up with Trina last night." I pushed a finger to his mouth when he tried to speak up. "I know you didn't, I trust you. Odd as that is coming from me, I truly do. I was trying to track her down so I could kick her ass for spreading rumors."

I could see his love for me when I admitted I'd finally given him my trust, and it made me feel horrible about what I was about to do.

"Listen, I um, I don't really know how to approach this, so I'm going to come right out and say it. I think we should take some time apart."

To his credit, he didn't react nearly as badly as I thought he would, and I wasn't sure if I should be grateful or bothered by it.

"Things happened so quickly with us. Maybe it doesn't seem that way to you, but it does to me, and I don't want to screw up. I know wanting to be apart probably doesn't make sense, and I want you to know I'm not running, I just...Before I fully hand my heart over to you, I have to know for myself that I can handle your... lifestyle."

"What does that mean? Is it because of my job? That it's dangerous?"

I couldn't blame him for being confused. I wasn't explaining myself well. Probably because I didn't fully understand it myself.

"No, no. I mean...*this*." I gestured around his house with my hand, my gaze landing on his pool, which had several occupants."

"Oh, you mean my house and the visitors? We don't have to-"

"No, let me stop you. I'm not asking you to change. I wouldn't do that, it's not fair. I have to come to grips with having to share you with so many people, and that's my hang-up to tackle. I'm not giving up, but after today with the rumors and finding Trina's naked ass in your room, it's just a lot to take in. It's *literally* the opposite of how I've lived my life, and maybe there is compromise somewhere for the both of us, but I need some time to figure it out."

"Okay."

"Trust me, I...wait...did you just say 'okay'?"

"Yeah, if you really think that's what you need, then okay. As long as you aren't giving up then I can live with giving you a little space."

He truly didn't seem bothered by my request, but it sunk in that he said 'little' space, and that's not what I was really asking for.

"I meant more than a little space. Some true time apart. I know it's not fair to you, so if you'd rather just throw in the towel now I'll understand." I would understand, but it would still hurt like a bitch.

"So...are you saying you want to see other people?"

I hadn't thought my stupid idea through enough. Of course it wasn't fair of me to cut him out of my life, even temporarily, and expect him to sit around waiting for me to work out my shit. Yet the thought of Joe sleeping with another woman made me feel so enraged that I probably could've bent steel with my bare hands.

"I don't know the answer to that. I know I don't want to see anyone else, but I also know it's not fair to expect you to be celibate. So I guess do what you feel you need to, but if things work out between us, I don't want to know what happened while we were apart. I don't think I could handle it."

The silence between us stretched, and I had to dig my elbow into my knee to keep my leg from bouncing. My nerves were getting the best of me, but eventually he let out a resigned sigh and slumped his shoulders.

"I'm not happy about it, but if this is what you need, then I can do it. Under one condition."

I hesitated, not really wanting to agree to a condition before hearing it, but knowing I was already putting him in such a shitty spot had me nodding my head in agreement.

"When you come to your decision, if you decide to give us a real shot, then make sure you are one hundred percent in. There's not a lot I won't do for you, Carrie, but being strung along isn't one of them. I know I can make you happy, but I won't make myself miserable in the process."

My heart lurched, and for a second I reconsidered my proposal. Knowing he was right and that it most certainly did look as if I was stringing him along made me feel horrible, but I wasn't playing games. I really did need time, and the commitment he was asking for wasn't one I could give him until I'd had this time to think things over.

"Thank you. I can promise you that I'm not trying to be difficult. I'm so sorry for this."

I already had regret brewing inside me as he walked me to his door, saying melancholy goodbyes before I walked to my car.

And with every step I took farther away from him, the more I hated myself for being too screwed up to just take a chance.

CHAPTER 15
CARRIE

"Why are you doing this?"

Two days had passed since I'd asked Joe for some space. Stacy had spent those two days hounding the crap out of me, reminding me over and over again how stupid I was.

"Stacy, please stop. You're making me crazy. I know you don't get it, but I have to do what's best for me. If I let things keep going the way they are with Joe and then decided later I just can't do it, it would hurt him way worse than me needing a little break now."

"Well I don't like it." Stacy crossed her arms and pouted, plopping down on my bed and watching while I packed. "So okay, whatever, you need space. Do you have to do it a billion miles away?"

"L.A. is hardly a billion miles away." I rolled my eyes, though my back was to her and she couldn't see it.

"Don't roll your eyes at me, smart ass."

"Oh my God, we've been friends for too long Stacy."

"Whatever, bitch, you love me." I glanced at her and saw her staring longingly at my little wardrobe closet that was storing anything and everything *besides* a wardrobe. "Soooo...you want me to get your mail for you and stuff while you're gone?"

"No," I scoffed. "I took your key away from you for a reason and you aren't getting it back. Plus, that wardrobe cost me a fortune and I don't want to come back and find it in pieces because you couldn't stand not being able to get inside of it."

"For someone with a closet full of sex toys, you are seriously no fun." I turned to toss another leotard into my suitcase just as Stacy was pulling out half of my packed bag.

"Knock it off!" I swatted her hand and she humphed in response. "There is no direct correlation between how fun someone is and the number of sex toys they own. Besides, if things end up working out with Joe, I won't need those anymore. His tongue does what no toy can."

"Dirty." Stacy waggled her eyebrows at me, then let out an exaggerated sigh. "How long will you be gone?"

I lost count of how many times she'd asked me that question since I told her I was leaving for L.A. "I already told you, I don't know. Could be a few months, maybe less. The club Reed is opening there isn't fully done yet, but the projected time line has them finishing in a couple months. I've got to do auditions and then get everyone trained before I can come back."

"Did you tell him yet?"

I didn't need to ask to know who *him* was. It was another question she already knew the answer to, so I didn't bother responding.

"You have to tell him, Care."

"I know that!" I snapped, tossing my hands into the air. My outburst would cause most people to rear back, but Stacy's ass backwards response was to crack up.

"My, my, you're testy."

I sighed and fell back onto my bed, curling into Stacy's side and throwing an arm around her waist. When we were younger we'd cuddle like that at night, mostly from fear of the dark or monsters under our bed. As we grew up, it became a comfort due to broken hearts or asshole fathers who abandoned their families.

"I'm not telling him until I'm about to board my plane. I wouldn't put it past Joe to show up at the airport with a boom box or stage a flash mob or something to get me to stay."

"Dammit, you suck the fun out of everything. You know I've always wanted to be in a flash mob."

I snorted and snuggled closer to her, my head laying on her shoulder. "I'm gonna miss you, but I'll be back here before you know it."

Stacy gave me a squeeze and pulled out from under me, turning on her side to face me. "I know; it just feels a lot like running. And I know I'm a selfish bitch, but I don't want to lose my best friend."

I held out my pinky between us, a proffering, which she reluctantly returned. Just like when we were kids and one of us needed reassuring that everything was going to be fine, and that one gesture was all we needed.

A month had gone by, and not a word from Joe. No text, no call, just...nothing.

I would have accepted this as his respecting my wishes, but my daily phone calls with Stacy confirmed my worst fear. Joe was fine. He wasn't miserable, not eating, depressed and crying over me being gone. He was living his life as his same old self, and that made me feel like shit for multiple reasons.

One, if you care about someone you should want them to be happy, right? So what did it say about me that I was so freaking upset that he was doing just fine?

And two, I was questioning why I did this in the first place. The distance wasn't affecting him at all, but I was a freaking mess. Wasn't I doing this so I could figure shit out? I was more confused than ever.

Stacy, always the butter-inner, had planted a seed in my brain that wouldn't quit growing. Like a weed it sprouted and used my insecurities as food for the cause, making me turn into the hot mess I was secretly wishing Joe was instead.

"You know, you shouldn't play games, Carrie. No one knows better than me," she'd said a few nights before on the phone. *"If you did this as some sort of test,*

*then that's fucked up. You can't do that to men, they are
clueless. If this whole thing was to see if he'd be a mess
without you, then that shit backfired because he's totally
fine."*

Never one to sugar coat things for you, I knew I
could count on Stacy to tell me the gut wrenching, soul
crushing truth. Unfortunately, I found myself wishing
she would just lie, or at the very least, play it down a
little.

I guessed it was possible that she was right. That
maybe I'd subconsciously hoped Joe would go crazy
without me, and that maybe that would be enough to
squash the remaining insecurities I felt. It most certainly
had not been at the forefront of my mind. I might have
been a selfish bitch, but I wasn't cruel enough to just
screw with someone for my own benefit.

Still, until I could figure out how to wrap my head
around everything and the possible ramifications of what
I'd done, I'd decided to quit taking her calls. I made sure
to send a text here and there to let her know I was alive,
making up excuses that I was sure she didn't buy one bit,
but I just couldn't bring myself to hear more. Every time
she told me Joe was 'just fine' I died a little inside. It was
slowly killing me, bit by bit.

I managed to get away with avoiding everyone for a
couple weeks, but that plan went to shit when a familiar
face walked into one of my sessions with the dancers for

Reed's new club.

"Ian!" I ran and leaped into my big brother's arms, unaware of how much I'd missed him until I saw his stupidly handsome face. "What are you doing here? How's Adalyn?"

"You'd know how she is if you'd answer my freaking calls," he admonished. I cringed outwardly. Ian's was probably one of the only opinions that actually mattered to me, and I hated the disappointment in his voice and knowing I'd put it there.

"I know, I'm sorry. I just couldn't hear any more about Joe and how freaking wonderful his life is without me." I'd meant to sound flippant, but it came out more bitter than anything. "I know; I sound like a spoiled brat. Don't worry, Stacy has made it perfectly clear how reprehensible my behavior is to everyone."

I expected agreement from him, but he was looking at me like I had two heads.

"I don't know what you're talking about, but you should know that Stacy's opinion has no bearing on my own. And anyway, that's not why I'm here."

"Why are you here then?"

"To spend time with my little sis. Six weeks is entirely too long to go without seeing my only family. I was going to plan an impromptu visit out here to surprise you anyway, and then a potential new client from L.A. requested a meeting, which worked out because now I get to expense it all as business."

His cheeky grin was ridiculous. "Ian, you're richer than God. A trip to L.A. is a drop in the bucket for you."

"I'm not quite that loaded, but the reason I have all that money is because I didn't spend it frivolously."

I rolled my eyes. Ian very much looked the part of the billionaire that he was, but behind the fancy clothes and very expensive facade, he was still just a normal guy. One of the main reasons anyone who met him loved him. Even Adalyn, who was more bitchy and stubborn than *me*, believe it or not, couldn't help but fall for his charms.

"So anyway, I see that I interrupted something. Are you free for dinner later? Maybe you can show me around while I'm here."

"Actually, we're just finishing. Give me ten to wrap things up and we'll eat a late lunch."

A few hours later, Ian and I were wandering around the city, teasing each other just like old times. It was making me terribly homesick, which knowing my brother, was part of some master plan to get me to come back.

"I've been waiting for you to bring it up, but you've been none too subtly avoiding the topic, so I'm going to pull the big brother card here and force you to open up to me."

I sighed, but I knew it was coming. He wasn't going to let it go, either. Once he made up his mind about something, he didn't stop until he got his way. Both an endearing and really freaking annoying quality to have in a brother.

"Fine, what do you want me to say."

"Level with me and tell me why you're really here. Don't disrespect me by feeding me some bull about it being a good work opportunity, or you needing to figure shit out. I know you better than that, and you know I'd never judge you, so tell me the truth."

We stopped walking and sat down on a bench just outside a little antique store on the main strip we'd been walking down.

"I'm scared." Ian furrowed his brow at me, as if to say 'duh'. "If it were just one thing that scared me, then I could handle it. But it's a lot of things. Everything. I hate feeling like I can't control the situation, or even my own feelings, and I don't even know where to begin to fix things."

"Have you tried talking to Joe about your fears?"

I scoffed. Ian knew me better than that. "Of course not, dummy. That would be the mature and logical thing to do, and I prefer to make my own life difficult and as miserable as possible. It's kind of my M.O."

It was Ian's turn to scoff.

"Well why haven't you at least tried to talk to *me*?"

I'd thought about it. No one knew my hang-ups bet-ter than Ian, because he'd lived through our parents' shitty marriage, too. He was right next to me when our dad walked out, never to be heard from again, and when our mom died after drinking herself into oblivion for years.

"You've got enough on your plate, Ian. Between your business and being a newlywed with a baby on the way...I didn't want to dump my crap on you like I always do. I thought I could handle this on my own."

Ian pulled me into a side hug and squeezed me tight before pulling away and putting his hands on my shoulders, his arms fully extended so he could look me straight in the eyes.

"That's the dumbest excuse I've ever heard."

I pushed him away teasingly. It was so frustrating how often he was right. "I know, I'm sorry. I've been making a lot of really stupid decisions lately. So many that I don't even know how to get myself out of this hole I've dug. I just don't want to end up like mom."

Shit, had I said that last part out loud?

Based on Ian's reaction, that would be a resounding *yes*.

"Correct me if I'm wrong here, but I take that to mean that you're afraid Joe's playboy status means he won't be faithful to you?" I nodded, uncharacteristically choked up and unable to speak. "You know Joe's nothing like dad." The tenderness in Ian's voice broke the dam, and for the first time in a very long time, I sobbed in my brother's arms.

"Carrie...I have a confession to make," Ian said after several minutes once my sobs started to die down. I wiped my eyes and looked up at him, then gripped the edge of the bench with my hands, predicting that I would need to brace myself for what was to come. "Dad never cheated on mom."

Well, shit. That wasn't at all what I thought he was going to say. Then I saw it. The guilt of the secret he was harboring, but I was already hurting too much to be angry with him, no matter what he said.

"A few years after mom died, dad contacted me. I ignored him at first, too angry to want to hear him out. When my business hit it's peak, and he contacted me again, I decided to face him. You and I were both doing well on our own, and a part of me wanted to shove it in his face that we weren't affected by his absence.

"I was almost too late. Dad was pretty much gone, the syphilis had taken over his brain and dementia had set in. His caregiver gave me a journal he'd written for us. I didn't even want to read it at first. I felt horrible for waiting so long to talk to him, and if what was in it was going to make me feel worse, I just couldn't face it."

Ian reached inside his jacket and pulled a small leather bound book out, and we both stared at it with fear - him afraid I would be mad that he was just now telling me, and myself afraid of what was contained inside.

I put my hand over his, gently taking the book from

his grip, and gave him a peck on his cheek. He startled and looked at me with disbelief, which made me laugh.

"Don't look so surprised, big brother. I'm capable of acting rationally once in awhile. My most recent behavior doesn't really set a good example for that, but I'm trying to be better."

Ian offered to be with me when I read it, but I declined politely. I wanted to be alone when I fell apart. And I was *certain* that I would fall apart.

After another few minutes of small talk, Ian could tell I was anxious to read what was inside, so we said our goodbyes with promises to see each other soon.

As anxious I was to read the journal, I forced myself to continue walking. I wanted to be in the right frame of mind to read it. Ian didn't outright tell me what our dad had written about, but eluded to it possibly being life altering for me. That was most likely the reason he'd kept it from me for so long. There was a time when it drove me nuts how Ian took it upon himself to decide what was best for me. Over time I've come to realize that more times than not, he's right. And the times when he's wrong, his heart was in the right place.

The sun had just gone down and the air had a slight chill to it, and I had my 'doh' moment. You know - the one in those stupid romantic comedies when the bloody annoying girl finally freaking realizes what the audience has known the whole time? The pivotal moment where she's already screwed up by being so damn blind, and it ends up taking some grand gesture to win back the man she loves?

Yeah, that was me. I was that girl who spent so much time being in denial, refusing to face reality, that she almost lost everything.

Only my life wasn't a movie. There was already a decent chance I'd done irreparable damage and it was too late. That there wasn't a gesture grand enough to bring back what I'd turned my back on.

I had always prided myself on being brave and taking risks - my love life being the one part of myself I had kept guarded. I used my parents' failed marriage as an excuse, among so many others that no longer held any weight. My fear of getting my heartbroken blinded me to the fact that it was breaking just by denying myself the happiness Joe was offering me.

Joe knew what he was doing when he let me leave. I had to decide for myself that I was stronger than the fear, and it was Ian's story of regret that finally did me in. Whether or not my dad had cheated on my mom was irrelevant to my decisions, because my life was my own. I was trying to avoid following my mom's footsteps by denying myself the potential to fall in love, but all I was doing was making my own life just as miserable as hers, only in a different way.

I would spend the rest of my life not knowing if I

could have fixed things if I didn't take the leap and find out. No matter the outcome, it was time for me to go home.

CHAPTER 16
CARRIE

I wanted to go straight to Joe when the plane landed, but I needed a shower and a change of clothes before I went to declare my love and put it all on the line. I thought it best to not smell like airplane funk when I saw him after ignoring him for almost two months. I made sure to put my dad's journal in my purse, wanting to have it with me, because I was going to be reading it no matter what. No more avoiding, no more denial - I was going to tackle life's hurdles head on.

I just hoped Joe would be beside me when I did.

I knew Stacy was going to ream me a new asshole when she found out I was back and didn't tell her, but I didn't want any distractions. Where the fear had once been, excitement and hope took up residence. I had spent my entire flight telling myself over and over again that even if Joe had moved one, that I was still going to tell him how I felt. If he didn't want me, then at least I'd know I gave it a shot.

By the time I got to Joe's house, I was so amped up with adrenaline that it didn't register that something was wrong until I got to the front door. I didn't bother knocking. Showing up without a heads up was the norm with Joe, and his house was never locked. The moment my hand wrapped around the doorknob was when I finally realized something was off.

Peering through the windows, my gut bottomed out. His house was entirely vacant. Turning in a full circle, I saw what else was missing; the normal slew of cars that took up half his driveway, the sounds of people laughing or talking drifting from behind his house. Then I saw the sign right in the freaking middle of his yard. A real estate sign with big bold letters across the front that said **SOLD**.

"Sonofabitch!"

NO ONE found it prudent to tell me that Joe freaking *moved*?!

Fury and panic extinguished my excitement. I was freaking pissed, and several someones were going to hear about it.

JOE

"She's going to kill you."

Chad's fear of Stacy was understandable. It was a fear we all shared. Only difference was I didn't have to suffer her wrath like Chad did, so I wasn't too worried about how she'd take the news.

"I think I could take her," I joked. Chad snorted. "Besides, I think all will be forgiven after the show."

Another snort. "You know, this whole 'snorting' thing you and Stacy have been doing is getting really freaking annoying." He snorted again, just to piss me off.

"You son of a bitch!"

Fuck. "Stacy," Chad and I groaned her name in unison.

I swung around on my stool where I'd been perched at our local watering hole and greeted Stacy with an over-the-top smile.

"Save your fake ass grins for someone who is gullible enough to buy your bullshit, because I sure as hell don't. You sold your fucking house?! What the hell, Joe!"

"I'm great, thanks for asking. Good to see you, too. How is your day going?"

"Can it, asshat. When did this happen?"

"Recently," I answered vaguely. She gave me her 'bullshit' look, but still moved on to the next question.

"You said you were renovating. What the hell has Chad been doing with all his time away from me if he wasn't working on your house with you? You said there were dangerous fumes and shit, and I was just dumb enough to believe you. So what the fuck?"

I threw Chad a look and pleaded for him to save me with my eyes, but he chuckled and pretended he didn't notice. *Dick.*

"He *was* helping me. Stuff had to be done to get it

ready to sell. I didn't tell you I was selling it because I didn't want Carrie to find out."

She eyed me with skepticism, like she was trying to decide if I was being honest. Which I was. Chad was helping me, and the house did need stuff done to it, but that's not what Chad was helping me with. Tricky wordplay for the win.

"Well, Carrie knows," she stated flatly.

"What the hell?! Did you call her as soon as you found out? Damn you don't waste time running your mouth."

"Screw you, jerk. She's the one who told *me*." She blew out an annoyed breath at my confusion and waved her hand in the air, like I was a dumbass for not being able to read her fucking mind. "She's back."

My back jerked, my whole body going alert. Carrie was back. Why had no one told me? Why didn't she tell me? How long was she back for? For good? Had she made a decision?

As if reading my thoughts, Stacy answered all my unspoken questions. "She didn't tell anyone she was coming back, not even Ian. I only know because she was pissed when she went to your house and found out you'd moved, and naturally she called to bitch me out like it was my fault that you'd lost your damn mind. She thought I was keeping it from her and didn't realize her asshole boyfriend was keeping secrets from everyone."

My ears perked up like an eager puppy at the word 'boyfriend'. Almost two months of not seeing her, feeling her, or even hearing her voice, and she still had me wrapped around her finger.

"Dammit, I thought I'd have some notice," I muttered to myself. "Okay, listen, I know you hate me right now and I swear I'll make it up to you, but you have to do me a favor."

"Damn straight you'll make it up to me, but that doesn't mean I'm going to do a favor for your lying ass."

"I'll tell you where Gerard is."

Chad growled behind me, but Stacy took the bait eagerly and offered her hand as an agreement.

"I need you to keep Carrie away from me, just for a few days," I rushed to explain. "I can't tell you why, but trust me it's not bad. Just keep her busy and away from places she might run into me. Okay?"

Not bothering to wait for an answer, knowing Stacy was just giving me shit and would do anything for me, I bolted out the door. As soon as my foot hit the sidewalk I shot a text to Chad and Ian, then headed to Grind.

"I know it's late notice, but she came back unexpectedly. I want to do this before she and I have a chance to talk again, and I have everything else lined up. The guys are ready, so if you can manage to pull this off then

I would owe you one huge-ass favor, redeemable any time you want."

Reed narrowed her eyes at me, and I knew I had her. Throwing the words 'if you can manage' in there had issued a challenge, and Reed never backed down from a challenge. I knew she could pull it off, it was just a matter of whether or not she *wanted* to.

She crossed her arms and tapped a manicured finger on her chin like she was contemplating taking on the task, but it was all for show. Reed may have been one hardass woman when it came to business, but she had a good heart and she knew the cause behind my request. She was the biggest donor for the community center, though all of her donations were private. I was the only one who knew where the money was coming from.

"Alright, fine. But you really owe me," she said with a pointed finger at my chest.

After making a few more phone calls, everything started to fall into place. As long as no major last minute hurdles came up, then in two days' time I would be making what romantics would call a 'grand gesture'.

I only hoped it would be enough.

CHAPTER 17
CARRIE

"I seriously don't feel like going out tonight, Stacy."

She didn't know it yet, but even after trying to talk myself out of it, I finally tried to call Joe. I'd wanted to talk to him face to face, but after spending hours driving around the city and not being able to locate him, I broke down. He didn't answer, and I was about to hang up - no way was I doing it over voicemail - when the automated voice came on. Only it wasn't a freaking voicemail message - it was some fucking recording telling me that his number was no longer in service.

The odds were against me, and my resolve was withering, but I refused to admit defeat until I'd talked to him. Of course, if he had moved and changed his number as a way of avoiding me, then that was a pretty big 'fuck you' message he was sending. I didn't know his reasons, though, and assuming the worst wasn't productive. So the best thing I could do was stick to my original plan.

I just hoped that didn't include having to hire a P.I. and stalk him, because honestly, I was to the point where I would actually do it.

I went back and forth between hoping for the best and assuming the worst. It was hard to ignore the signs that he'd most likely moved on. If he had, I'd let him go.

I'd respect what he wanted, no matter how badly it hurt. *After* I made an ass of myself with the little speech I'd written on the plane.

"Don't care, bitch. You've been gone for weeks, avoided my calls, came back without telling me and then bitched me out about Joe without so much as a 'hello, how are you'. So you're dressing your tiny little ass up in the hottest dress you have and we are going to Grind. And if you try to resist, I swear to all things holy that I will use Chad's handcuffs on you and duct tape your mouth and drag you there anyway. You know I will."

Yes, I did know she would. She would probably prefer it, seeing as how Stacy loved the dramatics more than she loved sex. Which was saying a lot. Unfortunately for her, I was not in the mood to put up a fight. I had other areas to focus my energy on, like how maybe someone at the club would be able to give me some information on how to contact Joe.

Speaking of which… "I'll go if you give me Joe's new number."

"Oh for fuck's sake...I already told you I can't."

My chest constricted and my eyes burned, but I refused to let myself succumb to old insecurities. Stacy cared about me, I didn't doubt that. But her loyalty to Joe's request, and her unwillingness to even explain why he was trying so hard to avoid me, was like kicking me while I was down.

In the past, the self-absorbed side of me would have thrown a tantrum until I got her to cave or avoided her out of anger. But the new and improved Carrie realized that Stacy wouldn't agree to something that would ultimately hurt me, and forcing her to betray a friend would be cruel and selfish. So I squeezed my eyes shut tight and fought back the tears, and focused on finding something to wear.

After an hour of enduring a very impatient Stacy nagging me to hurry up, I was finally ready. Decked out in my highest pair of hot pink stilettos, the shortest and tightest little black dress I owned and a simple pair of diamond stud earrings. I'd gotten my hair styled in L.A. and instead of my straight brown hair reaching my butt, it sat just below my shoulders in loose waves. Drastic eye makeup completed the look, and finally content with my appearance, I walked into the living room where Stacy was pacing the floor.

"Holy crap on a cracker."

I laughed at Stacy's reaction, my self-esteem going up a notch, because it was not easy to shock Stacy and I had. "You like?" I did a graceful turn to give her a look from every angle.

"Damn, if I was into chicks, I would totally hit on you tonight."

"Umm, thanks. Weirdo."

After a brief argument over taking a taxi, I gave

Stacy another win and got in the back of the yellow cab. I had no intention of drinking and wanted to have my car so I could leave if I found information on how to find Joe, but I didn't have enough of an argument without admitting that little part, so I gave up. I could always take a taxi back to my place and grab my car if I needed.

The club was busier than I'd ever seen it. If we hadn't had so many connections within Grind, I don't think we would have even gotten in. The shouts and groans from the long line outside the door proved how lucky we were to be let in right away.

"Holy shit, this is nuts!" Stacy yelled over the music as we made our way towards the bar.

"Hey guys." Adalyn pulled me into a hug before I had a chance to say hello back. Huggy Adalyn was still weird, but it was like she got more affectionate each time I saw her. What the hell was my brother doing to her?

"What the heck are you doing here? Are pregnant people allowed to go to clubs?" I asked as I returned her hug. I felt her laughter, rather than heard it, when her protruding belly jiggled against me. I pulled back and took in her form. She'd grown a lot in the time I'd been gone and was now visibly pregnant.

"Yes, but I have to admit I'm here under duress. I've not been feeling well lately but Ian made the biggest freaking deal about it. I figured he wouldn't ask me to get out in my condition unless it was important, so here

I am."

"Is he here?" I hadn't talked to Ian except for a quick text and I was eager to thank him for his visit.

"Not yet. He said he will be here in a bit. I wanted to just wait for him, but he practically pushed me out the door. He was behaving so oddly today."

Stacy was being strangely quiet, and Adalyn and I both looked over at her at the same time to see her staring down at her phone. When she looked back up she jumped a little, like she was caught doing something bad. Adalyn and I both crossed our arms, and unintentionally took identical stances with our bodies. We both knew how to deal with Stacy, and the only way to get her to fess up to a secret was to stare her down.

"I know nothing, I swear!" She rushed on when we gave her unbelieving looks. "Look, see!" She held her phone out for us to read the text she'd just received. It was from Joe, and just seeing his name on her phone made my heart rate pick up a little.

Get everyone to the front of the stage pronto. No questions.

Stacy was dragging both of us towards the stage before we had a chance to question her further. My eyes were darting all over, squinting through the mass of people trying to spot Joe. He must have known we were there, and if he wanted us in a specific location, then he was probably there as well. Which meant he and I were in the same place.

I suddenly felt like I was going to be sick.

The crowd parted and made way for us, opening like the red sea, and it was freaking bizarre. That's when I realized that almost every person in the club was staring at us. I wanted to shrink down and hide, but the possibility of Joe waiting for us - or maybe even me - kept my legs moving.

We reached the stage, and to my dismay, Joe was nowhere in sight. I was about to tell Stacy to text him back when suddenly every light in the club went off. It was pitch black, and dead quiet, and for a second I thought the building had lost power. That theory was quickly disproved when bright spotlights hit the stage, and the DJ started a mix of a song I'd never heard. It was catchy and the crowd started moving immediately, but every eye was locked on the stage.

A shadow appeared from behind the curtain, the spotlights aimed in just the right way to keep their face hidden, but you could tell by their build that it was a man. When he reached center stage, another spotlight kicked on, and my heart stopped. Staring directly at me was Joe, wearing his signature smile and some sexy ass pants.

Perfectly formed skinny black dress pants, sneakers and a white shirt. He looked so amazing and the girls had to literally hold me back when I tried to leap onto the stage. He pointed at his heart and then at me, in an over-the-top boy band type gesture, and the love in his eyes had tears streaming down my cheeks.

The beat kicked up and Flo Rida's 'Here It Is' came on, then Joe was moving. No, not moving...*dancing*. Son of a bitch, he was a good dancer. How had I not known that? I mean, he was no professional, but to the untrained eye he was pretty damn impressive.

I cupped my mouth with my hands and screamed for him as he moved effortlessly across the stage in a choreographed dance. When the first chorus came on, two more figures emerged to join him on stage.

"Holy hotness, Batman!" Stacy shrieked.

"Not Batman...Superman!" Adalyn corrected as Chad and Ian took spots next to Joe and joined in. They weren't as naturally gifted as Joe, but they still performed all the moves correctly and stayed in sync with each other. Chad and Ian had on similar outfits, only Ian's button down was open with a Superman tee underneath, and Chad's shirt was rolled up to show off his massive biceps.

By the second chorus five more men joined them onstage, all of which were my *own* dancers.

"What the hell!" I yelled and saw several of them wink at me. There was no way they heard me, but my face no doubt gave away my shock. It was clear they had been working closely with the guys and had most likely done the choreography for them. They had to have been working on it a long time, and judging by Stacy and Adalyn's equally surprised faces, they had no clue about any of it either.

When the song came to a close, all three of the very fit men were breathing heavily and sweating. The crowd went crazy, and a stage hand ran out and handed a mic to Joe. All three of the guys stayed on the stage, but after a few bows and waves the rest of the dancers left the stage. Joe took a few seconds to catch his breath before attempting to speak into the microphone.

"Thank you everyone for being here tonight. Me and my boys have been working on this for the last six weeks, and let me tell you...dancing is hard work. After this experience I definitely have mad respect for my girl, knowing she does this day in and day out. Speaking of which - thanks to the dancers at Carrie's Choreography for working with us. We couldn't have made this happen without them, and they were troopers, that's for sure. This grumpy ass gave them hell the whole time," Joe joked, pointing his thumb at Chad, who jerked his head in agreement.

"Special shout out to Reed and everyone who worked with Grind to help pull this together at the last minute. We've been planning this a while, but my girl showed up sooner than expected, so we had to get things moving quicker than anticipated, and none of this would have been possible without all of you."

It didn't go unnoticed that he kept referring to me as 'his girl'. I stood there staring up at him - all starry-eyed and love-struck - and I didn't even notice Chad and Ian walking over to me until I was gripped under my arms and lifted on to the stage. I glanced back after they plopped me in front of Joe in time to see them both hopping off the stage and pulling their women into their arms.

Then the room was spinning. My vision went blurry and my knees almost gave out. I vaguely heard the crowd cheering, but everything else dimmed and all my focus was on the man who was down on one knee. One hand held mine and the other held the microphone to his mouth.

"I know this is probably the last thing you expected from me, especially given the circumstances of the last two months, but I can't go another day without showing you how committed I am. To you, to us, to our future. If this is too soon, you don't have to give me an answer, but either way I'm not going anywhere. You're it for me, Carrie, whether or not you'll keep me makes no difference in the matter."

I stared in disbelief while someone appeared from backstage, handing him a little blue box. Joe didn't open it and hold out, asking me those four words that most women long to hear. Instead he clutched it between both hands, the microphone now laying on the ground beside him, as he waited for me to process everything.

"You...you moved. You changed your number. I haven't heard from you this whole time. I don't understand?"

I needed answers before I could answer him, because none of it made sense. He stood, taking my hands in his, though one was still holding the box. I didn't look at it, but I could feel it's smooth edges pressing into my palm.

I took a deep breath and closed my eyes for a second, relishing in the nearness of him. The familiarity of his scent, his touch. Everything I'd missed more than I'd even realized. When I looked at him again, tears flowed openly down my cheeks.

"I sold the house because I wanted us to have a fresh start. No strangers or uninvited guests. I only lived that way because I hated being alone in my house. It reminded me too much of when I'd been alone after my parents were killed. But you are all I need, the parties and everyone else don't matter. I changed my number for the same reason, so I could leave my past behind me and focus only on my future. It killed me not to reach out to you, but I wanted to give you the space you needed and make sure I was ready for when you came back. I know you probably hate all this attention on you, and me asking you to marry me right after you asked for space probably doesn't make sense, but I can't hide how I feel any more

Carrie. I love you, and I always will, no matter what you decide. There is no pressure, not from me. I just...I just needed you to know."

His voice was barely above a whisper, and the whole crowd had gone silent, though they couldn't hear his words from so far away. I looked around at everyone, taking a minute to absorb the moment, wanting to remember every detail.

Then I took a step back. His hands fell from mine and dropped to his sides, his face crumpling. I moved around him, and glanced over my shoulder to see his head hanging slightly and his shoulders slumped. Another look in the direction of my friends showed their disappointment, and Stacy was the only one who caught my wink.

I leaned down and picked up the microphone, held it to my mouth and faced Joe's back.

"Yes."

I spoke loudly, and laughed when Joe whipped around and scooped me up in his arms. The crowd stayed silent as he asked me to say it again.

"I said...yes!"

The room erupted with applause and cheers when his mouth claimed mine. I clung to his body, hopping up and wrapping my legs around his. It had only been a couple months, but it may as well have been years for how much I missed the feel of him.

He carried me backstage, still wrapped around him and our mouths never parting, and when he let me slide to my feet I whimpered, not wanting there to be any distance between us. With our foreheads pressed together, our noses touching lightly, we stood there and just breathed each other in. It was the happiest and most relaxed I think I'd ever felt in my life. I wasn't scared or over thinking things. I wasn't second guessing my every thought, emotion and feeling. I was just letting myself get swept up in the moment.

Swept up in the moment with my *fiancé*.

Holy crap, I liked the sound of that.

CHAPTER 18
JOE

She said yes.

Holy shit. I was engaged. I still couldn't believe it. Sure, it'd only been an hour so I hadn't really had a lot of time to digest it all, but still. A part of me thought she would run, or at least freak out a little. Maybe slap me or faint. I had no idea where her mind was, but I knew if I talked to her before the performance and she said she didn't want me, then I might never have had the courage to tell her.

It was worth risking the humiliation and the heart-break, because Carrie needed to know that someone loved her enough not to leave. Not to turn their back because things were hard, or because she needed to deal with things her own way.

"Hey, Romeo. Snap out of it and join us in the celebration," Stacy said as she handed me a beer. We'd all gone back to hers and Chad's to celebrate. I'd wanted to take Carrie home and celebrate in private, but there would be time for that. A lifetime of it.

"Well it's nice to know the reason behind all the secrets and lying. If I wasn't so awesome in bed, I might have been worried for a while there that Chad was cheating on me with all the time he spent away from me lately."

I laughed when Chad nuzzled Stacy's neck and whispered something in her ear that had her shivering. Never thought I'd see the day that my hardass partner and my playboy self would be so freaking whipped over our women.

"I still can't believe you guys got up there and danced, although it really was hot to see my Superman grinding his hips like that. All the women in the place were going nuts. Made me want to stake my claim in front of them."

Ian leaned over and rubbed Adalyn's belly. "I think my baby growing inside of you is staking your claim well enough, though I'd never object to you claiming me in other ways."

"So when's the wedding? As your maid of honor, I refuse to wear anything made of tulle or that has bows. Also, we sure as shit are going to have male strippers at your bachelorette party, so let's get that out in the open now."

"Um, wow. Slow your roll, there Stace. We've been engaged all of an hour and my fiancé is a known flight risk. Let's keep your usual antics to a minimum for a while, okay?"

Carrie punched my arm and gave me a mocking dirty look before turning the same look, slightly less mocking, to Stacy.

"June fourth. Pretty sure I get to pick my maid of honor, and I don't remember asking you. *If* you get to be in the wedding party, you'll wear whatever I damn well please. And hell yes, there will be strippers."

The room erupted. Stacy was going off about the maid of honor thing, Adalyn was already spouting out ideas for themes and colors, and Ian was stating his displeasure at the whole stripper thing. I stood there, dumbfounded and trying to wrap my head around the fact that in a few short months I would be married.

If I had my way, we'd just elope. I couldn't wait to call her mine, but I would do whatever Carrie wanted. Though based on the exasperated look Carrie was giving me as people bombarded her with ideas and questions, it might be pretty easy to convince her that eloping was a good plan.

CARRIE
ONE MONTH LATER...

"Thank you everyone for coming today. Before we get started, I want to give extra thanks to Adalyn and Carrie for helping me with this. Between the pregnancy and upcoming wedding, I know you're both very busy, so I truly appreciate it."

Seeing Chad stand in front of us delivering his

speech had both Adalyn and myself close to tears. Though, she had pregnancy hormones as an excuse. I was just a sappy nut lately. Falling in love had turned me into the kind of girl I'd always sworn never to be. And I was loving every minute of it.

I crossed my fingers and hoped Stacy wasn't going to say or do something stupid to ruin the moment. She was notorious for spouting her mouth at the worst of times, and seeing Chad shift uncomfortably and tug adorably on the neck of his shirt had me concerned. He was so obviously out of his comfort zone and looked like he could spook if someone so much as coughed.

I took a step forward and joined Chad, waiting for his instructions. It gave me a better angle and I could fully see Stacy's face. She looked like a cross between confused and scared.

"Anyway, I'll uh, let Carrie take over from here so you guys can get going."

Chad looked at the ground, completely avoiding Stacy's dramatic attempts to get his attention. I bent slightly at the waist to put myself in her line of vision and did my best to give her a 'sit still or I'll kick your ass' look. It must have worked, because she huffed and crossed her arms, but otherwise stayed put.

"Alright, everyone except Stacy head to your assigned locations. You know what to do. I have my cell so if there are any problems, text me, but make sure to speak in code in case my phone gets *stolen*." The last word was spoken with a pointed look at Stacy.

After everyone had filed out of the room, Stacy marched over to me. "Enough is enough. The last ten minutes damn near killed me, but Chad made some weird ass threat on the way here, saying if I didn't 'shut my goddam mouth for once in my life' that it would pretty much be the end of our relationship."

I almost fell over laughing. Chad deserved a freaking medal for putting up with Stacy all the time. Having to threaten her just to get her to be quiet for ten minutes was sad, but necessary. If I didn't love her so much, I'd have to wonder if Chad had some screws loose or something. Then again, I had my own quirks that Joe had to put up with, so who was I to judge.

"Okay, okay. I can tell you a little about what's going on." I paused for dramatic effect, and partially to piss her off, because having the upper hand with Stacy was too rare of an opportunity to squander. "Chad wanted to do something nice for you. God knows why," I muttered. "He has put together a scavenger hunt for you, and if you complete all the tasks, then it will lead you to Gerard."

Stacy squealed and jumped up and down like I'd just told her she got to spend the day with Ryan Reynolds, not go on a wild goose chase to find her vibrator.

She yanked the paper I was holding out of my hands, almost tearing it, and started reading the cleverly worded riddle that had taken me several hours to come up with. I was a dancer, not a poet, but I was proud of the little clues I'd come up with. Hours spent putting together rhymes and using wordplay, looking up synonyms and brainstorming with Adalyn about location choices. All that time spent, and Stacy had it figured out in two seconds and was already running to the car.

Luckily my lack of creative ingenuity didn't seem to spoil the fun for Stacy, which was made obvious by her bossing me to 'quit driving like a snail on Ambien' the whole way to the bakery. Ten minutes in the car with Stacy and I was already regretting going along with Chad's plan. I loved her dearly, but she could suck the fun right out of shit with her obnoxious personality.

After passing Stacy along to Ian, I made my way to the final destination. Chad was nervously pacing inside the jail cell at the station where he and Joe worked.

"Everything's going great, Chad. You should try to relax a little." He looked at me like I'd lost my mind. "Seriously. Nothing you say or do is going to get her to change her mind if this isn't what she wants, so stressing is useless. She's having a great time already, you did good."

He scoffed and sped up his pacing. "You and Adalyn did most of the work, I just sat around like a putz."

I stepped inside the cell and put a firm hand on his shoulder, which wasn't easy because he was more than a foot taller than me and built like a professional football player. He didn't resist, luckily, or I might have been bowled over.

"You don't give yourself enough credit," I said affectionately before pulling him into a hug. Neither of us were the touchy feely type, but Stacy was like a sister to me which made Chad an honorary brother, and he needed to be reassured, even if he didn't know it.

My phone dinged with a text from Joe. "She's on the last one. Should be here any minute." Chad's response was to break out into a sweat. Only Stacy could get the strong and stoic Chad to lose his cool, and it never failed to surprise me every time I saw it happen. Looking at him you would think nothing would rattle him, but Stacy could win a war with her bitchy attitude alone. When Stacy went off on a tangent, you could see the crazy in her eyes, and Chad had been on the receiving end of it enough to get a little freaked out.

Ian and Adalyn came into the precinct just a few minutes before Stacy came bursting in with Joe hot on her heels.

"Listen, fuckers. If this was some elaborate plan just to put me in jail, then I'm going to be pissed. Gerard better be here somewhere!"

Stacy's eyes searched the room, as if her missing vibrator would be out in plain sight in the middle of a police station. Her eyes landed on Chad, who was standing stock still, frozen with his eyes wide. He looked absolutely terrified, and my eyes naturally darted to Stacy, who was looking at him like he was crazy.

"Uh, whatcha doin' Officer CrazyPants? You grow a conscience and suddenly feel the need to turn yourself in for stealing my private property?"

I'd asked Chad in the beginning if he wanted us there for the big finale, thinking privacy would make it easier, but he said he wanted witnesses. Why? In case she attacked him. In a police station. When he, himself, was an officer.

Dear God, my friends were crazy.

When Chad didn't so much as move a muscle, let alone respond, Stacy stomped over to him. Chad took a step backwards with one leg, and started to bend the other, but was interrupted by a commotion happening behind us. I almost ignored it, assuming it was just an officer bringing in someone who was causing a scene, but it wasn't. It was worse. *So* much worse.

Adalyn's very pregnant body was lying on the ground, and though Ian and a couple officer's were blocking my view, I could see she was out cold.

All I could do was stand back and watch as Joe and Chad forced everyone to give them room while they called for a medic. Everything after that passed in a blur. It felt like seconds later that a still unconscious Adalyn was being loaded into the back of an ambulance with my very upset brother climbing in behind her. Joe ushered me to his truck and drove me to the hospital - neither of us saying a word the whole way there - with Joe holding my hand tightly and squeezing every few seconds for reassurance.

By the time we got up to the maternity ward, Adalyn was already in the back being seen by a doctor. When Chad and Stacy walked in my attention was briefly shifted to the ruined proposal Chad had been working so hard on. Minutes that felt more like hours ticked by, and when Ian came bursting through the doors we all leapt to our feet at the same time.

I threw my arms around my brother, hugging him for a few seconds before pulling back. The worried look on his face made my stomach drop, and I held my breath, praying everything was okay.

"First of all, Adalyn is okay." He paused and we collectively let out a long, relieved breath. "She had what's called placental abruption. She's not far enough along for them to deliver the baby, though that would be ideal since it's very life threatening for both her and the baby, so they will be keeping her here until she is at least thirty-four weeks so they can attempt delivery."

It wasn't great news, but she was okay. Ian made it sound like it was no big deal, but several Google searches later told me a different story. It was a really serious condition, something that could easily have cost her her life if everyone hadn't reacted so quickly. Ian told us we wouldn't be able to see Adalyn for a while, so I offered to go to Ian's house and get him some things. He didn't have to say it - there was no way he was going to leave her side. He'd probably be there every minute of the few weeks they would have to wait before delivering.

"I'm sorry guys, I know this is probably the worst time to do this, but after the scare with Adalyn, I can't put it off a second longer."

Chad immediately fell to one knee, in the middle of the maternity ward waiting room, and thrusted his hand in the air towards Stacy. She stared at the little blue box, dumbfounded, and after an absurd amount of time Joe cleared his throat to break the silence. Chad shook his head slightly, as if to clear his head.

"Marry me."

Not a question, not followed up by the romantic speech I knew he'd been rehearsing. Chad said it like it was a command, and I really expected Stacy to smack the box out of his hand and tell him to go screw himself for barking an order at her. Instead she dropped to her knees in front of him and pulled him into a hug, and though I couldn't hear it, I knew she was sobbing based on the shaking of her body as he held her.

Joe, Ian and myself quietly slipped out of the room to give them privacy. With a promise from Ian to call if anything changed, I reluctantly left with Joe to go fetch

Ian's things.

I was visibly shaken by the events of the day, and it was dark by the time we got to Ian's house. On shaky legs I made it to the couch with Joe's help. I hadn't cried yet, but I was on the verge and was sure Joe could sense it.

Slowly pulling back from him, I sniffled and wiped away an escaped tear, then pressed my lips firmly to his. When I pulled back, I touched my forehead to his and took a deep breath.

"I don't want to wait."

His thumb stroked my cheek, and he gave me a tight lipped smile. "Today got everyone shaken up, but maybe you should take some time to think about this. Maybe sleep on it."

My eyes widened, and the words were out before I could stop them. "Oh my God, you've changed your mind." Frayed nerves had me acting irrationally, but luckily Joe was still sane, and he pulled me back to him.

"Stop, you know that's not the case. I'd do it tomorrow if you'd run away with me, you know that. I just don't want you to rush into it. I want to give you the wedding you deserve."

I shook my head adamantly. I understood his concern, but he was wrong. "No, I want to marry you now. Whether we do it tomorrow or in two months makes no difference, I won't change my mind about wanting you forever. I can't spend the next two months planning a wedding with my sister in law in the hospital, and furthermore, I don't want to. The wedding isn't what matters to me, it's the reason for it."

He eyed me for a while, like he was trying to figure out if I understood what I was saying. "What are you thinking of then? Eloping? Your brother would want to be there."

"No, I don't want to be that far away from them while Adalyn is in the hospital. I want to see if we can get someone to do it at the hospital, in Adalyn's room. I want everyone I love to be there, so let's take the wedding to her."

Joe smiled lovingly at me, before stepping out to make some calls while I packed Ian's bag. I was so happy, knowing I would be taking the next step with Joe sooner rather than later, that I didn't even flinch when I had to stuff my brother's underwear into an overnight bag. *Black silk boxers, Ian? Really? Ew.*

SEVEN MONTHS LATER...

"How the hell did they talk us into wearing these stupid ass costumes?"

"Shut up, Chad, you love it."

"Actually it was Joe's idea," I chimed in, earning myself a glare from my husband. Even six months after exchanging vows in a dimly lit hospital room that smelled like antiseptic, I still couldn't get over knowing I was married.

Joe had managed to pull off the ceremony in two weeks' time, a week before they ended up delivering my new niece. I wore a simple white dress and the men wore suits. I'd brought Adalyn a beautiful hand-made blanket to cover herself with in her bed so she wouldn't feel dressed down, because they wouldn't let her change out of her gown. Stacy, however, wore a thrift store dress I'd scoured the city to find. It was straight out of the 80's and was peach colored with shoulder pads and was almost one hundred percent tulle.

It was her worst nightmare and she bitched the whole time, even grumbling to herself during the vows. The whole ordeal last five minutes and there were nurses coming in and out of the room to check on Adalyn during the short span of time it took for me to marry the man of my dreams.

It was perfect.

"What the fuck? *It was Joe's idea?* Why the hell would that motherfucker want to go to a costume party dressed as one of the *Three Amigo's*?"

"I think you guys look really handsome," Adalyn said as she walked in holding a bundle of baby perfection.

"Gimmegimmegimmegimme!" I all but yanked my

niece out of her arms. "Hello princess," I cooed, melting a little at the gurgling sounds she gave in return. "When do I get one of these?"

Joe smiled and looked jokingly at his watch. "Ummm, six more months? Ish?"

"What!? I didn't know you guys were trying! Congratulations!" Adalyn was closest to me and the first to pull me into a hug, quickly followed by everyone else. Everyone except Chad, who was still throwing a tantrum over his costume.

"How the hell did I let you guys talk me into this? I seriously look like an idiot."

Joe clapped him on the shoulder, unphased when Chad shoved him away. "Stacy asked you in the middle of a really awesome blowjob. *That's* how you got talked into it. Stop thinking with your dick, dick."

"Where did you find those costumes anyway, Care?" Adalyn asked absent mindedly while she changed a diaper on the couch.

"I had a seamstress who does costumes for my studio all the time make them. Cost me a small fortune, but was totally worth it. They look like they stepped right out of the movie."

"I get to be Steve Martin. He had all the game," Joe joked before breaking into his own rendition of "My Little Buttercup."

"Did your seamstress do our costumes too?" Stacy

was fiddling with the belt on hers before pulling on her shoes.

"Yep, she's the best."

Ian walked into the room and handed Chad a shot glass. Ian was as excited about the costumes as Joe, and Stacy had confided in us that Chad was secretly excited too. He was just too macho to admit it.

"Don't you think it would have made sense for the women to dress up like us?"

"You want me to dress up like one of the Amigos, too?"

"You know what I mean, Stacy. Like in dress like Carmen wore in the movie." Everyone froze and looked at Chad, who misunderstood our inquisitive looks. "What? You know, Carmen - the daughter of the village leader and was trying to find someone to fight El Guapo for them?"

Chad just kept digging his hole the longer we stared at him.

"Aha! I fucking *knew* you loved that movie!" Stacy pointed her sword at him victoriously. "You try to act like you hate those costumes, but I saw the limited edition copy of it hiding in your DVD stash. It's a fucking classic, so stop acting like a dick and just get into it already."

Chad looked nonplussed, but then Ian and Joe stepped on either side of him, and the three men did a perfectly timed 'Amigo Salute.' It was, hands down, the most awesome thing I'd ever seen. It should have been absolutely ridiculous, but the three of them were so fucking hot they somehow managed to make it look cool.

"What are you guys dressed up as anyway?"

Ian looked at Chad with disgust. "Seriously? You can't tell what they are? They're Wonder Woman."

"It takes three women to dress up as one person? I don't get it."

"Oh my gosh, you're hopeless." I loved when my brother went 'Nerd' on someone. "They're different version of Wonder Woman. Adalyn is Artemis, Stacy is Orana and Carrie is Queen Hippolyta."

"Dude, the only thing that explanation just clarified for me was how big of nerd you are."

"Hey, don't know why this just popped into my head, but did Chad ever give Gerard back to you Stacy?" Everyone groaned when Adalyn threw the question out there. Based on her smirk, it appeared she was intentionally trying to rile things up.

"Okay, you know what? I've had it. You want to know why I took Gerard from Stacy?!"

"Chad don't…"

Chad ignored Stacy's plea and kept on with his tirade. "She tried to use it on *me*! Yeah, you heard me. She tried to shove that thing up my ass, and I'd had my limit! I let her get away with a lot of freaky shit in the bedroom, but you don't cuff a man to the bed, blindfold him and then try to shove a rubber dick up his ass. She agreed to get rid of it if I swore to never tell anyone, but I'm done being blamed for the loss of her precious sex toy!"

Chad's chest was heaving up and down and his face was bright red. He looked like he was going to explode. Or have a stroke. Stacy looked mortified, and even my little niece had ceased her cooing. It was totally silent, aside from Chad's harsh breaths, until Joe cleared his throat.

"Well, that shit's going to be ingrained in my head for the rest of my life. Thanks for the mental picture."

Everyone filed out of the room silently, Joe and Ian tense and uncomfortable, while Adalyn and I were biting back laughter. By the time we made it to the first floor of Ian and Adalyn's new house, the guests were starting to arrive. Adalyn handed over the bundle in her arms to the nanny who would be helping during the party, and Chad and Stacy came down the steps tentatively.

"Did you guys kiss and make up?"

"Fuck you, Joe," Chad bit out.

Bickering ensued between the group, but I just stood back and looked on. We were all certifiably crazy, and would probably ending up paying a small fortune to put our future children through therapy. Life would never be boring for our ragtag group of crazies, that much was certain.

And I wouldn't want any other way.

THE END, BITCHES!

ACKNOWLEDGEMENTS

Oh, where to start!?

The more I publish, the more people I have to thank. I've made so many wonderful friends and connections in this journey, and I'll be forever grateful. If I miss anyone, it was not intentional, please accept my deepest apologies and feel free to throat punch me in the future if necessary.

First I want to thank anyone and everyone who took the time to read my books. Whether it was under coercion, or of your own free will, I am honored. Especially those of you who took the time out of your busy lives to leave a review online, good or bad.

Secondly, thank you to all the authors who continue to inspire me. Samanthe Beck - When I started stalking you, I never dreamed I'd get to call you friend. You put up with my crazy and have offered support and mentoring I never would have expected. Your talent is a level I can only aspire to reach one day. http://www.samanthe-beck.com/

Can't forget my family! Continual thanks to Susie and Monica for their proof-reading talents. You guys are an integral part of my support system, and without you I would suffer greatly!

Mommas - Your faith, encouragement and unending support is amazing. Even though you skip over half my book because of the language or "dirty" parts, I still love you for even trying.

Jenny - You may be a bloody twat, but you're still one of my very best friends. One day I'm going to fly to England and tackle hug you for all your support and friendship.

To the girls at Bare Naked Words - Thank you for assisting me with my very first blog tours and helping to answer all my questions and offering your support. http://www.barenakedwords.co.uk/

To Booksmacked Blog - namely Melissa - You are one awesome bitch. I don't think anyone else in this whole process has taught me more than you have - mostly about social media, promoting and marketing, but also for proving me wrong on the whole Canadians being passive bullshit. You're the bossiest, most straightforward person I've ever met. https://www.facebook.com/BookSmacked/

Last, but definitely not least, thank you to my hubby. Not many authors are married to their cover designer / web developer / formatter / publisher / everything-else-under-the-sun. You're my best friend, an amazing spouse and the greatest father to our children. Nothing I've done over the last 11 years would have been possible without you, and that's just the facts. I love you.

To anyone I missed, I love you, thank you, and goodnight!